A Dandelion on the Roof

AND OTHER STORIES

Georgina Scillio

Clouds of Magellan

Australia

© Georgina Scillio 2008
First published 2008
Clouds of Magellan Publishing
www.cloudsofmagellan.net
All rights reserved

ISBN 978-0-9802983-8-3

A National Library of Australia Cataloguing-in-Publication record is available for this title.

Cover image: Rosemary Bell
Design and layout: Gordon Thompson
Printed by Trojan Press | www.trojanpressbp.com.au

This collection won first prize in the Clouds of Magellan / Northern Notes Writers' Festival (City of Darebin) Pitching competition, sponsored by Trojan Press, Thomastown.

 **TROJAN**

Georgina Scillio (nee Zammit) was born in Malta and migrated to Melbourne when she was twenty. She lives in Fairfield and is married to Reg. They have three sons, Mark, Simon and Julian and four grandchildren, Juno, Cassia, Leonard and Daniel.

Contents

3 ~ Shafts of light

To Concetta Zammit Schembri, my beloved mother, for her courage, strength and rock-solid Faith.

Acknowledgments

To my dear friend Marietta Elliott-Kleerkoper for her encouragement and advice over so many years. To my wonderful writing group friends 'The Cartridge Family'. To Gordon Thompson, Ashley Sievwright and Helen Bell of Clouds of Magellan for their support and assiduous editing of my stories, and to Trojan Press and the Northern Notes Writers Festival (City of Darebin) for sponsoring and supporting this publication. To my dearest husband, Reg, for his love, patience and continual support.

1

Malta

Rosa's Wedding

One summer evening, we were playing in the *cul de sac* which was our street, when suddenly there was darkness.

It was Rosa, falling from the sky—her large, navy blue cloche skirt opening up like a parachute above us, momentarily causing an eclipse of the sun. Rosa threw herself from her balcony on the second floor. We learnt later that her boyfriend had migrated to Australia and her parents had refused to let her follow him.

Fortunately for her, Rosa did not land on her head, but on her bottom, and even more fortunately, she did not fall on any of us, or we would have been crushed to death by her substantial weight.

I secretly liked Rosa a lot and was quite jealous of her. She was an only child and quite pampered, unlike us who were poor. Not only was she so much older than us—she must have been eighteen or so at the time, and that by itself was perceived as a great source of power— but she was also a free spirit. Rosa wore her hair piled high on her head with lots of hairpins, which made her appear taller and, in my eyes, smarter than anyone else I knew.

She wore high heels and fishnet stockings with a dark seam straight up the back of her legs. I promised myself that if I could not afford fishnet stockings like hers when I grew up, I would paint a line along the back of my legs, to pretend I was wearing them. I wanted so much to be like her even though she was considered to be a bad girl by some of the adults.

THE WAR HAD JUST ENDED and the underground bomb shelter in the middle of our street had been sealed, its entrance now guarded by barbed wire. Inside that dark, dank and roughly hewn shelter, the people had spent days and nights hiding from the enemy planes as they pounded us with shells for four years. Some of the children were born in that shelter. There were people who had survived the bombings, but died instead of terror—their hearts stopped at the sound of the bombs raining on our Island.

Now there was peace and our parents were pleased. At least we could play, if not in complete safety, then without the shrill sounds of air raid warning sirens interrupting our games.

The war had left us with a strange toy: the gas mask. There had been a big scare that Hitler would pour toxic gases on us. Hitler kept his poisonous chemicals. We kept our masks—green and black rubbery things with two large hideous mica lenses, which would provide us with much amusement. We wore them and chased each other around the street. The boys would wrap sheets around themselves and chase us girls in the dark to frighten us. We played *il-Hares*, the dreaded ghost, or *ix-Xitan*, the devil, while running around and screaming.

The mothers yelled from doorways, balconies or windows, 'Watch that baby! Keep away from the barbed wire!' But to no avail. The games would only stop if someone got hurt or we'd collapse from exhaustion. Sometimes, a father would appear, take off his belt and threaten us with a spanking, and we would scurry away to our houses.

But we felt safe in our crescent-shaped street, with the noisy comings and goings of sellers of vegetables and fish, and occasionally, *gelati*. Although our knees and elbows were always bleeding, or had thick scabs which never healed because of our meagre diet, we thought this was the best place in the world. It was an extension of our houses.

There were women feeding their babies on the doorsteps, or picking out lice from their children's hair, or removing the little stones from the rice spread on their laps. They all kept an eye on us.

From the pulpit of the Great Basilica, our parish church which, unlike the buildings around it, had been miraculously untouched by the bombings, Dun Karm continued to confuse me with his pedantic utterances. God was a fulminating angry old man who was ready to pounce upon us at the least misdemeanour, for, not only were our sins of commission and omission writ large in his Book, but our bad thoughts as well. Had I not stolen pennies from my mother's apron pockets, and swallowed a mouthful of water as I washed my face, when I should have been fasting completely from the previous midnight before receiving Communion? Had I not wished that Mary Mifsud, who had bullied me to death in our games, would be trampled to death by a horse and cart? And was not that heinous thought the same as if I, with my own hands, had pushed Mary under the galloping horse? Had I not wished, too, that a balcony would fall on Pietru who, unprovoked, had pushed me onto barbed wire, tearing my best dress as well as my flesh?

In the end, having considered myself as a lost cause, my mortal sins so grave and gross and my soul irredeemable, I decided to ignore the sermons and concentrate on examining instead the magnificent frescoes on the domed ceiling of the Basilica. Sitting on the uncomfortable straw seat of a chair, I tilted it so I could observe the images better,

3

ignoring the disapproving comments of the women behind me.

And if there was something that could totally transport me into paradise, as if bypassing all hurdles, it was the roses, painted on the handsome hemisphere of the ceiling. Their curved petals, their velvetiness—which even some hundred feet above my head I could almost touch—their sepals and leaves as fresh as if they had been washed by rain, was enough to make me feel ecstatic. How I would have loved to paint like that!

Then there were the rich robes and brilliant hues of the gigantic figures of Moses and other prophets. How did the painter capture the folds of silk, the light and shade of those extravagant garments to make them so believable? And what about the textures of the bearded faces of the old men, contrasting with those smooth cheeks of the angels?

Years later, when I visited the church and looked specifically for those roses, I realised that they were small, peripheral to the large images of the prophets and other religious personages. How over-heated my childhood imaginings were! But decades later, the gigantic figures of Moses and of the Virgin with Archangel Gabriel still appeared impressive, even to my cynical adult eyes.

Around the semicircular base of the dome, in letters grand and golden was written ECCE ANCILLA DOMINI FIAT MIHI SECUNDUM VERBUM TUUM. Later on I knew their meaning: 'Behold the handmaid of the Lord,' they said. 'Be it done unto me according to thy word.' Even before I went to school, no books at home to teach me the alphabet, I used to marvel at the incomplete roundness of the letter C, as if the artist had run out of gold paint and left it unfinished; and was bewitched by the perfect symmetry of the M. And I was awed by the serpent-like qualities of the S—Satan in the Garden of Eden, who we knew so much about. Even in church he was there, ready to put occasions of sin in front of us. But best of all, I adored the scintillating stepladder of the A, with its promise of a glorious ascent into heaven.

Around this time in my childhood, as if by some magic, four books, or rather four fragments of books, appeared in our house. They had been found among the ruins of a prosperous house, but they were so tattered, so stained, so incomplete, that no one must have wanted them. Except my mother, who brought them home and put them on her Singer sewing machine as if they were, even in their derelict state, handsome trophies to be looked at and looked after.

'When you go to school, you will be able to read these. Not like your father or your mother. You will not be a donkey like us,' she told me several times.

Il-Vangelu ta' San Mark, *Gray's Anatomy*, Manzoni's *I promessi sposi*, Dickens' *David Copperfield*—all without covers and most of their pages missing. They were to be the beginning of my love for books.

WHEN ROSA CAME OUT OF hospital limping on crutches, we all went to greet her. She told everybody, with her usual imperious manner, that she was going to follow her lover to Australia. To their great distress, Rosa's parents had been forced to give their consent, provided she married him by proxy first. This was nothing new in our village: dozens of girls had been married by proxy to migrant men they hardly knew, or had never met. The notion that the bride and groom were separated from each other by thousands of miles on their own wedding day had become quite acceptable.

On Rosa's wedding day, there were garlands of stephanotis, basketfuls of tuberoses and white geraniums, gardenias, and jasmine, jasmine everywhere. Entire summer crops of white flowers had been picked to decorate the reception room for Rosa's marriage. The bridegroom was in Melbourne, but the bride had his wedding ring. The priest said everything in Latin, but we knew all the responses. Rosa's mother sniffled and cried right through the ceremony. Not only was she going to lose her daughter to a man she did not like, and who was not even present at his own wedding feast, but he was going to take away her darling daughter to the other side of the world.

But we had eyes only for Rosa, resplendent in white tulle and guipure lace, although still on crutches.

There were *biskuttini tal-lewż* and sweets of every kind, and even for us children there was alcoholic anisette, diluted with water which turned it milky. I must have got intoxicated because I had to be carried home to bed before the party finished.

The next day I was told that Rosa had already left for Melbourne. I had not had time to say a proper goodbye to her, and her departure from our neighbourhood caused such grief in me that I was sure I would die.

A Dandelion on the Roof

One of my daily tasks is to hang the washing on the roof. I have to get the large enamel bowl full of wet clothes up three flights of narrow steps. The last ones are so narrow that when my mother is pregnant, which is almost always, she is unable to fit through them. I have to make several trips because I cannot possibly carry all the heavy washing in one go.

Lately I have been looking forward to going up on the roof. Every now and then a seed somehow finds its way into the cracks of the stone, and if the conditions are right, it will germinate and start growing. I have noticed to my immense delight that a dandelion plant has been growing in the crevices just outside the balustrades. It has two flowers on it. One is yellow and has just opened, the other is fluffy and white, ready to fly away.

How I wish we had a courtyard, or at least a few flowerpots in the balcony! This plant, this weed, this precious little friend, is the only green thing in our street. Only Censa's house has a courtyard and indoor plants. No one else has the time, the money or the patience to grow any plants here in this little horseshoe-shaped street of ours.

Some streets are lucky, they have pots in their windows, geraniums on their balconies, even vines in their courtyards. But here, in the *cul de sac*, there is nothing.

I had been watching the dandelion buds frequently just before they had burst into bright yellow, velvety flowers. I am so happy. Yet I am so worried that someone might come and pull them away, or that the wind will blow them off. I have kept this little secret to myself. I am hoping that mother has not seen the plant from below. She might want me to pull it out to give it to the rabbits.

Dent-de-lion, or lion's tooth, is where the name came from, I later learn in my Botany class. The French also have a nickname for it: *pisse en lit*, because of its diuretic effects when a tisane is made from it. Dandelion is a weed, a ubiquitous species, a broad-leafed pest forever being pulled out of the ground by those who desire smooth lawns. But it is almost indestructible because of its tap root. Its pappus of hairs with its multitude of seeds form a living parachute to disperse far and wide and propagate themselves away from the parent plant.

For me it is a cherished and dainty object of loveliness.

Instead of hanging the clothes, I go straight to where the dandelion is growing. I stick my head between the balustrades. I touch the soft, downy flowers, and I am filled with delight. I shut my eyes, and feel their smooth softness. I know the ephemeral nature of such raptures, because the dry cruel wind will soon blow away these delicate things of beauty.

I try to disengage my head from between the balustrades. But I am unable to do so. I try several positions. I try to remember how I had managed to get my head there in the first place. But the more I panic, the less I am able to recall at what angle I stuck my head in there before. I move my head around between the curved and corroded stones of the balustrade, in a kind of frenzy. But to no avail.

The sun is beating on my back. I am terrified that I may have to stay like this forever. In spite of the heat, I shiver at the thought that I will have lizards crawling over my body, ants biting me mercilessly, wasps stinging me to death. My heart is pounding in my chest. Mother is calling me from downstairs, impatient for the second lot of clothes to be hung. If you wait any longer, she yells, these clothes are going to dry in the basket.

She does not know that the first lot is already almost dry. This would make her mad, as they will be so creased that no amount of ironing will smooth them enough. She yells again and I don't answer. I am crying quietly to myself, hoping that something might distract mother so she'll give me more time to extricate myself.

It is quiet in the street below—it is too hot for anyone to be walking around. Behind me, the chickens in their enclosure are lying still, their wings are spread so as to keep as cool as possible. While I am standing here, trapped, I realise that I still have to change the water, and clean the chicken coop floor. I detest cleaning the chicken coop floor, especially with the rooster around. He is asleep now but he will get aggressive if I try to go near him.

Then, after what appears to be an eternity, I manage to pull my head out, jerking and twisting my neck painfully, and I cry out loudly with relief at being freed. The chickens wake up in alarm and start shaking the dust off their feathers. The rooster starts crowing, his huge plumed tail displaying itself in full glory while the hens around him cower, frightened.

The postmeridian silence of our street has been shattered. It is all my fault.

Have we not been warned against the danger of putting our heads through balustrades? Have we not been admonished about the damage we can do to ourselves? I do not tell mother of my experience or else I will incur a severe scolding.

I quickly hang the clothes on the lines: I have to stand on an old wooden box as I cannot otherwise reach the line.

Towels with towels, nappies with nappies. Bloomers and underwear together, hung at the back, so they cannot be seen from the street. Don't hang colours with whites or the whites may get stained. Don't push the pegs too hard into the clothes, or they will leave an unsightly mark. Straighten all the garments before hanging, or they will be full of creases. Turn the frocks inside out or the sun will bleach and discolour them. Make sure that the fly buttons in your father's trousers are all done up properly or the garments will be completely warped when dry.

So many rules. I try to always follow them. The consequences of not doing so are not very pleasant.

A Brief Sojourn in Paradise

I was giddy with excitement as I entered my Primary School for the first time. The white sandstone building, surrounded by a garden of hibiscus trees lush with brilliant red flowers, was the most beautiful school in Malta. My grandfather had had a part in its construction and I was very proud.

'I'm going to love it here,' I said to myself.

But I was one of the few pupils who had not learnt English, and during lessons I was totally lost. I knew some words like on, under, table, chair, window, and a few other simple ones. When the teacher kept saying to the class 'Understand?' I had no idea what I had to stand under.

My first weeks at school were hell. We were not allowed to speak in the corridors and we had to walk in single file on the black line painted on the floor. Most of the school was out of bounds with rules and regulations written in English, and threats of punishment about everything. The quadrangles were large enough to run races in, skip rope and even fly kites, but we were not permitted to run during either recess or lunchtime.

One day I strayed into a part of the school which was forbidden to us, and walked straight into the headmistress, Miss Buttigieg. I had no idea I was trespassing and I must have further aggravated the situation by wishing her 'Good Afternoon'.

'Go to my office immediately, you disobedient child!' she shouted.

I had interpreted this as an order to go back to class, and was heading in that direction when, enraged, she grabbed me by the arm and pushed me all the way to her office.

What happened later in her office is inscribed in my mind as some kind of crazy nightmare—she, big and bosomy, speaking to me mostly in English, my runty little self answering her tirades in Maltese. With great disdain she turned to the matter of my uniform.

'You realise that you are not wearing the proper skirt? It's not the right colour of navy blue for a start,' she told me in a mixture of Maltese and English.

'My cousins wore this skirt,' I told her, 'so why is the colour wrong?'

'Do not answer back, child!' she yelled. Couldn't she see that it had simply faded after so many washes, I felt like saying, but kept my mouth shut.

'Also, the pleats are too wide!' Miss Buttigieg told me, grabbing hold of my skirt and fanning it to show the offending pleats.

She gave me a lecture, and as the words tumbled from her mouth, I gathered that if she let this kind of misbehaviour go, the pleats would get larger and disappear, and before long we'd be wearing short and tight red skirts, wouldn't we?

'Can I please go now, Miss Buttigieg? Please!'

But she ignored my plea.

Next thing I knew the cane was being brought down from a cupboard and landing on the back of my legs. *Twang, twang, twang.*

The pain was excruciating, but I was too proud to cry.

'That'll teach you to obey the rules, you shameless child. Already, at such a young age, you are showing wicked ways,' she said, her face distorted with rage.

She then detained me for two more hours, which I had to spend standing in her office. But what hurt more than the welts on my legs was the humiliation of watching the other children file past and call out in one ingratiating voice: 'Good afternoon Miss Buttigieg!' the girls smug in the security that their fully pleated navy blue skirt bestowed upon them, and the boys sniggering at me surreptitiously, glad it was me and not them being punished by 'Madam'.

In our class there was a boy, Bertu Micallef, who tormented us girls, stuck his tongue out at us, and made rude gestures behind the teacher's back. He blew snot on our clothes, and made loud farting noises with his mouth, then rearranged his face quickly so that some-one else would get the blame. But Bertu had blue eyes and fair hair, so he could do no wrong. His father was in Australia and had sent him colour pictures of Australian animals of which we were very envious. During an assembly Miss Buttigieg told him in sugary tones,

'We will hang those lovely pictures of the koala and the platypus in the foyer, Bertu, for all the boys and girls to see!'

One day Bertu told us that he knew a magic trick that would double the number of our pencils. As we each had only one lead pencil for the whole year, this offer was very tempting. We handed over our precious pencils to him and he lined them up on the floor. He then closed his eyes, uttered an abracadabra, and jumped on them with all his might. The pencils split into several small pieces which were useless. It broke our hearts, but the teacher brushed it off as a silly prank we had participated in anyway, and she just let him off with,

'You naughty boy, Bertu, how would you feel if I did that to your pencils?'

'Dad will send me some more from Australia!' he replied cheekily, showing no remorse for the unhappiness and trouble he had caused us.

One night I developed a fever so high, I was delirious. I was hot and I could not swallow. I saw my mother and sisters in a haze—they were talking to me but I did not know what they were saying. I lost all sense of time. Was it yesterday or tomorrow? I knew the doctor had come because I had felt the cold metal of the stethoscope on my chest, and seen a dark moustache bending over me.

I heard my mother crying, and saw her sponging me with cool water. I fell asleep but woke with a fog in my head. Everything around me was blurred and had lost its edges, and all I wanted to do was sleep.

When my fever passed, it was decided that the best place for me to recover fully was in Nanna's house in the country. I do not know how long or how sick I had been, but I had become so scrawny, and my clothes were so loose that they seemed to belong to somebody else.

It did not matter, because I was in paradise. At night I slept in Nanna's bed, with its fragrant sheets and embroidered pillows. Each morning, she picked blood red oranges from her orchard, squeezed them, added a large spoon of golden honey, and gave it to me to drink. She tiptoed around the room, arranging the curtains so the light would not hurt my weak eyes.

'You're getting more colour in your cheeks, darling,' she would say constantly.

When I got stronger, I started following Nanna all day. I was not asked to scrub or sweep floors or make beds or dust furniture.

It was late spring and in the flower garden the colours and the perfumes made me dizzy. Since my mother was not around to disapprove, I ran after butterflies, chased grasshoppers and played with ladybirds. We would have lunch under the shade of the pomegranate tree, with Nanna fussing around and chattering away.

'Remind me to boil some sage leaves for you, little one.' Or, 'We'll pick some chamomile flowers today and let them dry in the sun.'

Now that life had taken such a heavenly turn, I decided that I would try to avoid going back to school ever again. I would hatch a scheme to stay here forever. I'd rather be dead than see the faces of Miss Buttigieg and vile Bertu ever again.

But one day Nanna decided that I was well enough to go back home. I pleaded with her, begging her to let me stay. But she was firm: 'Your mother needs you, and you have to go back to school.'

'No, no, no, I hate school and they hate me.'

I pleaded in vain, but I did not throw myself about in rage and frustration as I was likely to do at home.

Nanna took me firmly by the hand while I, dragging my feet and crying quietly, walked beside her. I was filled with dread at the prospect of returning to school.

When we got home the situation was worse than I had imagined. Mother was her usual harassed self. But this time her hostility was aimed at me. Dad had been away for weeks, eking a living in the salt pans, and when he came home he was too tired to do anything to help her with five small children.

'While you were having fun and being spoilt at Nanna's, I never had a moment to myself! Look at my hands!' she snapped at me.

The next morning, wearing a uniform that was too short and a little tight, I was taken to school by my mother, protesting and bawling my eyes out. At one time, she momentarily let go of my hand and I ran away. As I turned a corner, I dashed past the bakery, hoping to elude her. But she followed me screaming at the top of her voice: '*Aqbadli dik it-tifla*, catch that little girl!'

The baker's apprentice ran out and grabbed me, triumphantly handing me over to my mother, my navy blue skirt covered with flour.

I had been away from school for so long, that I was placed in a different class, Miss Galea's. She was very pretty and petite, wore pink twinsets made of soft and fluffy angora wool, and necklaces of shiny white pearls. She spoke softly to us and smiled a lot.

In the afternoon, we were too tired to write, so Miss Galea taught us about 'The World'. But for her, the world was England, and England was the world. She was a walking encyclopaedia of Britain. She described to us the lushness, the mountains, the streams and the forests and her voice rose and fell as if following the hills and valleys. While she painted the cool misty autumnal mornings in the British Isles, in the sunny afternoon somnolence of the schoolroom our eyelids would begin to droop, and our heads to nod. We listened enchanted, as if in a dream.

To us England belonged in the same domain as Jack and the Beanstalk. Most of what Miss told us was so delightful because it was a myth. The pictures she showed us of Englishmen in tweed suits smoking pipes, and stroking their daughters' pet puppies were as mythical as fairies drinking out of acorn cups. They had as much substance as Miss Muffet's tuffet, whatever that was.

The afternoons drifted off, on air, as it were, with Tom and Ann munching apples under English oaks and Jersey cows mooing over Devon downs. At times, harsh reality brought us crashing back to earth.

'He's done it again, Miss,' Spira Gatt would shout. She would be referring to Sammy Fenech, the boy who always walked around with a semicircle of wetness on his pants. The class would stop listening to Miss, and turn to look at the puddle of pee under Sammy's desk. At times, as he was being taken to the toilet by another boy, Sammy would cast a shy, almost conspiratorial glance at me.

The *purtinara*, the janitor, a dragon of a woman, came and mopped up the puddle, grumbling to herself.

Later, the *purtinara*, would arrive again with the dreaded codliver oil in a large tin. She placed it on a chair at the end of the corridor and we lined up to get a spoonful of the obnoxious stuff. We brought our own spoons and a slice of lemon, which was supposed to take the awful taste away. There was no escape from the codliver oil ritual, which the Maltese government had added to our school lives.

After that unpleasant break, we rushed back to our seats for more fairytales about cool evenings on rolling English hills and daisies on meadows, while the last drops of cod liver oil on our spoons putrefied in our warm school bags.

At the end of the lesson Miss wrote several new words on the blackboard for us to copy and remember. I became an avid collector of fancy words. The more she gave us, the more I wanted. I was becoming a sponge for words.

At about this time, I made a wonderful discovery: a discovery so simple, and perhaps so obvious, yet it was to change my whole attitude to life. It began to dawn upon me that beyond the world I inhabited of hunger and illness, rejection, and mother's moods, there was another much richer world of the mind. Even from my limited vantage point, that world appeared without boundaries, like the sky on a cloudless day. For how else could I be so transported by a picture, or by a story, to another place, another country, in such an effortless way?

I began to realise that I had to improve my reading because there was a universe out there beckoning me. Though I was too poor to even catch a bus to the next village, my imagination could travel much,

much further away, and I could return in an instant, and no one would have been the wiser.

Now I was beginning to like school a lot more.

One day I summoned enough courage to venture into a part of the school I had never been before and saw an open door, and on it a sign LIBRARY. I stepped inside. It was dark and cool in there. I had not seen so many books before. The walls were covered with shelves and there were no spaces at all on the shelves.

When my eyes adjusted to the dim interior, to my great surprise, I saw Sammy Fenech. He had an open book in front of him, and he appeared too absorbed to see me. From the window behind him, the diffuse light reflected from the red hibiscus flowers cast a certain glow on the boy, this rejected boy. I had never seen him so content, so at ease. I knew then that he, too, had found solace in words.

NINA

NINA'S YOUNG LIFE WAS SPENT falling in and out of love. In fact she could not remember a time when she was not in love. It was like being in love with the notion itself, because Nina loved from a distance, and was even content to remain unnoticed by her loved one. Being in love was not just an escape from harsh reality, but it also gave her a reason for being. Each time she fell in love, she did so deeply and intensely, forgetting the previous young man as if he never was. So it was not surprising, therefore, that after her infatuation with the picture of a German soldier ceased, and his image faded completely from her mind, someone else came into the picture.

On the way to the market she had to go past the police station. And there, under the blue lantern one bright morning, was Ganni dressed in a smart new khaki uniform. He looked young and fresh, for he still had not started to grow a beard. She had seen Ganni so many times before, but never in this light. And just at that very moment she noticed how blue his eyes were, how strong he looked, and how curly his hair under his hat. He must have just joined the police force, and he appeared to be very pleased with himself, standing there against the grubby granite façade. And from then onwards Nina invested Ganni with all the lover-like qualities of her previous loves, because, like them, he was now a man in uniform.

There was nothing in the world which excited her more than a young man in uniform. For a man in uniform had a job as well as status, and a man in uniform did not go round on bended knees grovelling for work. A man in uniform had a steady wage, a firm future, an orderly life and clothes without patches. A man in uniform had all the things her father did not have and more. And men in uniform had a certain assertiveness about them, a kind of confidence, at least in her mind, none of which her father had ever possessed.

And Nina's heart was full of young Ganni in uniform, and while she hung clothes on the line, or scrubbed the floor, or took her little sisters for a walk, he was a song in her mind. At least Ganni was not forbidden fruit like the German soldier, and she could see him alive, in the flesh, not just on a crumpled page of an old magazine. In her dreams she was his dutiful wife, and she bore his children and she slaved for him as if nothing else mattered, and no sacrifice was big enough.

But Mother strongly disapproved of daydreaming. '*F'dan il Wied tad-dmugh* (in this valley of tears) there is no rest …'. For her the only way to survive was sheer and constant hard work.

'I met Sinjura Grima today, and she's in a bad way with her asthma, and her poor husband in his condition. I want you to go and lend her a hand with the housework.'

Nina's entire day was spent helping others, and she never had any time for herself.

Nina, come and rock the cradle, I'm tired. Nina, go and get me a loaf of bread from the baker. Nina, I've spent all morning standing in the ration queue, and I've got a headache. Please take the children for a walk.

Most times Nina did not mind, but even when she did, she would never have dreamt of saying no. Being one of the older girls in the neighbourhood, she had to run most of the errands, helping mothers with their children and old people with their chores. She had never known any other way of life. Sometimes they gave her sweets, or a few pennies, or maybe even a dress, but most times people forgot to give her what they had promised. Some would let her have dinner with them; others fed their own children, while she went on with their housework.

As far as she was concerned, there were things to be done, and she did them. There were women with eight or more kids, and others on the way. There were toddlers and babies and children crawling everywhere and they all had to be fed and kept clean. She did not mind looking after children, she herself being in so many ways as guileless as they. Nina understood their prattle, and when they cried, she knew what they cried for, more so than their own mothers at times. And when they fought among themselves she did not lose her temper and hit them like their parents often did, for in many ways she identified with them more than she did with grown ups.

But Nina did not much like going to Sinjura Grima, for she was a sour woman who lived in a large dark house with her invalid husband. The house was on the main street where most of the wealthy people lived. But the Grimas had fallen on hard times, and now that they could not afford any servants, they had to rely on their neighbour's help.

'I don't want to go to Sinjura Grima's place,' said Nina. 'Her house smells musty. She never opens the windows and I'm scared of her husband. He just sits there, dribbling at the mouth and making horrible gurgling noises. I can never understand what he wants to say.'

'Don't worry, he's harmless. Oh, he was such a good-looking and nice man before the accident!'

Everybody in the village was sorry for Sinjura Grima's husband after his tragic fall. He was painting a fresco on the church ceiling when he lost his footing and fell from the scaffolding, some sixty feet from the ground. No one knew exactly how it happened, for no one had been around when he fell, and he never spoke after that. Some said that he had heard an air raid warning, and, terrified to be up there on his own, he hurried and slipped. He was not killed outright because his fall was cushioned somewhat by a stack of straw chairs which served as pews in those days.

Now he lay like a child, completely dependent on his wife and the neighbours, like so many people whose lives had been wrecked by the war. Angelo Grima had been an artist, a painter, much in demand. He could work magic with colours and plaster and his church frescos were beginning to be quite renowned, even in Italy where he had learnt the skills. The war had been a great blow for the Grimas, for their yearly pilgrimage to Italy was now a distant dream, as that country was now the enemy. Anyone expressing sympathy with Italy was deported to North Africa

But now Angelo's hands were useless. He could do nothing for himself, and when he needed something, he would weep or emit a guttural noise, and when he was angry or upset he would knock his head against the bedpost.

Their house had a small garden, but these days it grew mostly weeds. It had been completely neglected, with the rubble and rusty pieces of barbed wire and bits of twisted metal which had been thrown in during the war. In summer, a big apricot tree cast its shadow on the yard, and in winter, it stood sullenly by, surveying the desolation and the chicken house. Sinjura Grima kept chickens for fresh eggs, and when a hen grew old and tough, one of the neighbours would kill it for her to make soup for her invalid husband. She had tried doing that herself once, but she forgot to disembowel the fowl before putting it in the hot water. The resulting brew was horrible.

Chickens also made a mess and a smell, and brought flies if one did not clean their pen, so Nina was sometimes called in to help. Sinjura Grima had once given her a cake which tasted awful, for it was made without sugar as her ration of sugar had run out at the time, so Nina felt obliged ever since to help clean the chicken pen. And while she was there, she might as well sweep the house, wash the window panes, and dust the walls.

This time she realised that if she went to Sinjura Grima's place by a different and longer route, she would not only kill a bit of time on the way, but also pass near the police station. Who knows, her beloved policeman might be there, she reasoned. So, as always, in spite of her initial protestations, she obeyed her mother.

Sinjura Grima stood around giving orders, something she was very good at, for having been brought up with servants ever since she could remember, ordering people came to her very naturally.

Nina, don't forget the dust in that corner over there! You've forgotten that cobweb! There's a pool of water under that chair, you'd better go over the floor again.

And so on.

But the worst job of all was cleaning the chicken pen when the chicken dirt had hardened, layer after dry layer stuck to the ground. And she had to sweep it bending down as the roof was low and the hens kept flying up and down in fright and making an awful noise and raising dust, for these hens were kept inside all the time, or they would have flown over to the neighbours. Nina had to make sure that she did not trip over the water bowl, or hit her head against the roosting perch.

This time Nina noticed that there was a big rooster among the hens. When he saw her, he ran amok, flapping his wings, and pecking the hens with all his might. Then he started chasing her, and terrified, she knocked the water bowl and stepped on an egg that had just been laid. She ran out the door in fright and the rooster followed her, but as she slammed the door with all her might, the rooster's head got caught between the door and the jamb. He emitted a most frightful noise, and died instantly, with his head turning black and floppy, and his beak wide open as if in supplication.

To make up for her crime of killing the rooster, she had to go and help Sinjura Grima again and again, till the woman considered herself appeased. This time, moreover, Nina had to clean the bedroom where the sick man lay. It was a revolting task for there were all sorts of spit and slimy objects on the floor and on the walls. And Sinjura never offered her a drink nowadays, so she often felt weak and dizzy.

Nina would have loved to just sit in the shade of the apricot tree and dream of her beloved Ganni who would, one day, come and deliver her from this bondage.

Hunger

On those summer afternoons of my childhood in Malta, the searing heat melted the asphalt, and the blinding afternoon sun forced its way through the decrepit French windows. The corroded hinges and peeling stucco had witnessed not only two world wars, but the antics of the Knights Hospitallers themselves. In the shimmering heat, ornate brass doorknockers in the shape of dolphins, reminders of more prosperous times, appeared as if on fire at that hour of day.

But afternoons also brought us some respite from the relentless demands of the household, because to survive the punishing heat, we children would lie down on a sheet spread on the cool terrazzo floor, trying to have a siesta.

Soft images of dogs, and occasionally people, walked inverted on the cracked and crude plaster above my head, with the window slats acting like pinhole cameras. They entertained and amused me, captivated me, those figures on the ceiling. I wished that one day I would get up there and fill them up with colour. Like those magnificent figures on the domed ceiling of our parish church.

But, for our mother there was no rest. Since our father had been killed by a landmine before our youngest brother was born, mother was our sole breadwinner. To me, she was omnipotent, omnipresent, and omniscient. Mother was large and solid and, especially compared to my runty self, seemed like a mountain. When she took her breasts out of her bodice to feed the baby, they almost engulfed the child beneath them. At breastfeeding time, we knew instantly that we had to go tiptoeing somewhere else to do some task, if we were to avoid incurring her displeasure.

While the baby slept, mother would sit at her Singer sewing machine, looking grim and determined, pedalling furiously.

One memorable occasion, mother had to finish a piece of work for a difficult client, the *sinjura*. The *sinjura* would always complain no matter how perfect the design, or how well the piece was finished. Although I was only little, I felt sure that it was a cruel ploy to lower the already miserable price the *sinjura* was paying for so much labour.

As usual, the ice-cream boy's cries shattered the postmeridian quiet of the street. 'G-i-l-a-t-i. Ice-crea-ea-ea-eam!'

'Please, ma, can I buy an ice-cream? Please, please!' I cried and begged and pleaded.

'C-o-o-l, c-o-o-l, ice-cream!' the boy's voice taunted, but it was becoming fainter and fainter as I watched the ceiling shadow of the boy and his handcart receding along with my hopes of getting an ice-cream for the day. Another desire dashed. Two ice-creams cost the same as a loaf of bread to feed us all for a few days.

'Maybe next time!' Mother did not even take her eyes off her sewing, as she tightened the hoop around the floral patterns, threading the needle in a flash, trimming the edges with a pair of fine scissors, and then resumed her pedalling of the sewing machine.

'But you said that yesterday, and the day before, and the day before that!' I retorted bitterly. My eyes were filled with tears, sore and hot from rubbing and crying. My persuasive powers were as nothing in the face of mother, a megalith intent on her embroidery.

Perfectly parallel lines of white cotton tacking covered the soft, silken material which was part of a whole set of bed furnishings for *is-sinjura*. Ambidextrously, my mother tacked with her left hand, while with her right hand she inserted the padding under the slippery satin. I watched her, envious of her speed, her skill, but also of her authority over me and on all the things around me. I felt helpless and powerless as I wallowed in self pity.

Then the baby started to stir in his cot—an improvised hammock made up of old sheets hanging across a corner of the room. I swung the cot and its contents vigorously, almost with spite, the baby's shrill cries demanding immediate attention.

The *sinjura* did come and, to mother's joy and surprise, loved the ensemble. But no, sorry, she was not going to pay for it just yet. Maybe next month. Her husband was a sea captain and was away at that moment.

For us, not getting any money was a terrible blow, but almost expected. I was not allowed to be present in the same room when the *sinjura* came to collect her goods. But, from behind a curtain, I could see her—high heels and expensive fishnet stockings with a seam at the back of the legs, hair perfectly coiffed, lots of jewellery, bright red lipstick and nail polish. No woman in our street could afford to dress like that. I could also overhear most of the conversation with my mother trying unsuccessfully to hide her anger and the *sinjura* in her city accent, high-pitched and unnatural to my untrained ear, promising to pay as soon as her husband, *il Kaptan*, was back home.

That evening mother boiled some beans and cabbage and we ate the watery *brodu* quietly with all that was left of a dry loaf of bread. There were no more eggs from the chickens. We had eaten our last chicken a week ago. The rabbit hutch behind the kitchen was empty. Our last rabbit was cooked months ago. By the end of the evening there was absolutely no food in the house—not a slice of bread, not a lettuce leaf, not an olive, not a teaspoon of sugar. Nothing.

No, not exactly. In the medicine cupboard, high up on the wall of the bedroom, with a red cross crudely painted on it, I knew there was a packet of Aspro. When everyone was asleep, I got up stealthily and moved a chair underneath the medicine chest. I opened the catch slowly. There were still some tablets in the old, tattered, packet. That packet had lasted us since the end of the war. I took one tablet and started sucking it slowly, relishing its acidic flavour. I then went down the chair and back to bed, trying not to disturb my little sister Josie who shared my bed.

Before long I was up again to take another tablet, noiselessly sucking it till every single acidy crumb was dissolved in my mouth. I did this several times till there was nothing left in the packet. Finally, I put the packet back, exactly as I had found it, only this time it was empty. I was feeling drowsy enough that the thought of my mother's anger was quite dulled in my mind. And most of all I could sleep and forget about the gnawing pangs of hunger in my belly.

The next morning, I woke up with terrible blisters in my mouth and an insatiable thirst. Of course I never said anything about it, preferring to suffer in silence, rather than incur my mother's disapproval.

A few months before this, mother had made a dress for a relative whom we called Aunt Grezz, and she still had not paid us. So next day mother sent me and my sister Josie to ask Aunt Grezz if she could give us the money she owed us, as we had nothing left in the house. Mother sent us about lunchtime, I think with the hope that auntie might give us a bit of lunch while we were there. Aunt Grezz had a son who came home from work to have lunch. We had heard that they often have ham and cheese sandwiches for lunch. We had only seen ham in the shops, and had never yet tasted it.

Their house was in another part of the village, so it was a long walk in the heat. We walked across fields and through deserted war-ruined houses, carefully avoiding anything which might have contained a landmine, till we finally reached the newly built area where our prosperous relatives lived.

Aunt Grezz had some kind of a disability which made her repeat every word at least three or four times. We had often felt like giggling in her face, but mother had warned us that if we did that, it would be the end of any sewing jobs from her.

There was also something else about Aunt Grezz. Her face was so pale, that her skin was almost transparent. She looked as if there was no blood at all flowing in her veins. I had secretly suspected that her speech impediment was due to her great pallor, and it was a mystery to me how someone who had so much to eat and drink was always so ill. We hardly ever had enough food in the house, yet our mother had such a ruddy complexion, and was so much more lively and energetic.

When we arrived, Aunt Grezz was making a large *granita* for her son. We watched her making it, our eyes ready to fall out as we gazed at the cloudy glass with its mountains of green, lemony ice—soft, cool mountains whose transience in the dry air of auntie's kitchen was a source of breathtaking wonder for me. I closed my eyes conjuring up the heavenly delicious feeling of cold ice on our parched bodies. It would be like dying and entering paradise. Instead, I heard myself say politely,

'Mother sends her regards.'

'Her regards, her regards, regards, regards. She sends her regards. Marta, Marta Marta, Marta sends her regards, her regards. Good, good, good of her, of her, of her. Very much, very much. Please excuse the untidy kitchen, untidy, untidy kitchen. The untidy. You understand I have not been well, not well, not well at all.'

Looking around her spotless, her completely tidy and dust-free and modern kitchen, with everything precisely in its place, we did not know what to say.

For a few moments we just stood there hoping that she would offer us a glass, a sip, a touch even, of the *granita*.

Instead, she took out an embroidered doily with coloured beads sewn around the edge, and proceeded to put it over the glass in the centre of the large dining table. *He mustn't have any flies in his granita, her son, her son, any flies in his granita. Her beloved son. Her sunshine, her sun of God.*

There was no point in us staying. I pulled Josie by the arm, and whispered that we must leave now. There was not going to be any offer of *granita*, let alone ham or bread. Not to mention money. Auntie's eyes had momentarily illuminated the deathly pallor of her face at the sight of such polite children who had just dropped by to convey their mother's best regards. But she showed no signs of offering us any food, or at least a glass of water. She did not even invite us to sit down, but continued to mill around the kitchen and to set the table for her son, completely ignoring us. We felt that to broach the subject of unpaid money at that moment would have been the depth of rudeness.

Instead, we left, disappointed and confused. To go straight home to mother and incur her rage was unthinkable. So we started walking home taking the long route along a country road, which was at that time of day completely deserted.

Going past one of the fields we noticed that there was an apricot tree with one of its branches hanging over the stone fence, like the arm of some rich gypsy covered with large, gaudy gems. The branches were full of apricots. But the apricots were still hard and unripe.

Josie and I hitched up our skirts, climbed the fence, and started to pick every single apricot off the branch, eating each one of them and filling our pockets with their stones. 'One day,' I told Josie, 'we will have our own apricot tree. It will have fat, luscious, juicy apricots, and we'll have so many that we would be able to give away to all the poor children.'

Josie could hardly speak. She was sick. Doubled up. Our bellies were hurting terribly.

But that was as nothing compared to our mother's scorn and anger that evening. Why, oh why, had we not asked Aunt Grezz about the money that had been owed to us for so long?

The Competition

One day, we are brought to the school hall and are herded silently to sit in straight rows. We do not dare to turn our heads, to move a muscle, let alone chatter or giggle. We have been told to bring all our pencils and rubbers with us.

'Good morning boys and girls!' Miss Buttigieg's voice is unusually sweet today. She is up on the stage. From where we are sitting, her large figure appears gigantic, powerful, terrifying. Her eyes sweep across the hall. I am thankful that I am almost hidden in the end row close to the wall.

'Today, as you all know, you are to participate in a competition. A drawing competition!' She pauses for effect. I breathe a sigh of relief. At least we haven't been brought here for a mass humiliation, something our headmistress is famous for. Oh, I can redeem myself, I can draw very well, I am so thankful my mother bought me a set of coloured pencils at some great sacrifice. She worked long hours at the Singer sewing machine making some garments for the neighbours, so that I could have this box of coloured pencils. And I have them right here. I am very excited, but first I must pay attention to the instructions.

In front of each of us there is a sheet of white paper, thick, parchment-like, which the school has provided.

'You have all been listening to the broadcasts on the radio in the last few weeks, and you all know by now that today we are celebrating the anniversary of Hans Christian Andersen.'

There is a slight stirring of children in their seat, excited at the prospect of a competition. I have not heard of Hans Christian Andersen—we do not have a radio at home—but I am sure she will tell us all about him.

'You must all know by now the delightful stories of the wonderful Hans Christian Andersen on the Rediffusion! So today I would like you to draw a picture from his stories. And the boy or girl who wins, will get a set of lovely coloured books by the Brothers Grimm.'

I wait with great anticipation for precise instructions. My English has improved a little now, but there are many words that I do not know, I just try to guess their meaning.

'This row of boys and girls over here will draw *The Ugly Duckling*, those in the second row will draw *The Red Shoes*, next row will draw *The Little Match Girl*, and,' indicating where I am sitting, 'that row over there will draw a picture of *The Princess and the Pea*.'

No sooner has she finished talking than all the children put their heads down and start drawing, rubbing out mistakes, scraping away on the thick white paper. I am still completely bewildered. I do not know the story of the Princess and the Pea. Today is the first time I have heard of any of these tales. All this information must have been given when I was absent from school.

Miss Buttigieg starts walking around and I am petrified. I pretend that I am drawing and cover my picture. I have not the slightest idea what to do, who the Princess was, or what she was doing with the pea.

The only Princess I know about is Princess Elizabeth of England. She is up there on the wall with her family, a portrait made when she was a little girl, looking so pretty. It must be her, they are talking about. I try to peer at the desk in front of me, and the boy, as if reading my thoughts, immediately covers his page. No one is looking at the picture of the Royal Family hanging on the wall.

I make a rough sketch with a grey lead pencil, then I begin to draw in the details. First the head, the curly hair with the sweet little hat. The hat has a satin bow. There is an upturned brim, so smart, I would give my little finger to own a hat like that. I proceed with drawing the body, the arms, the dress. First an outline, then the details. The lucky princess is wearing a pale blue jacket and pleated skirt of some soft woollen material. She is standing straight between her father, the King, and her mother, The Queen.

The white gloves are a little tricky to draw. I use a very light grey instead of the white. The princess is wearing white socks, so I use the same colour for them too. I use my black lead for the shiny patent leather shoes. It is difficult to obtain the shine on this thick paper, but I try to match my colours as closely as possible to those in the portrait. If only I had more pencils, but I am getting her likeness. I am particularly pleased with the buttons on her jacket: my position so close to the wall means that I can see the minute details clearly. Each button has four tiny holes where it was sewn. I can even draw in the thread holding each button.

I am so pleased with myself, although I am a little worried about the pea. How am I going to depict it? Was she eating a pea? But princesses do not eat in public! And why only one pea?

Then I have a flash of inspiration: naturally it was a sweet pea plant! Grandma's sweet peas twine around all over her garden. I close my eyes and try to remember: the papery flowers, the keel shaped petals, the tendrils. I have a very bright red pencil and I use it for the flowers. It makes a nice contrast to the blue and white. Princess Elizabeth would like that: the red, white and blue.

I only have a few minutes to finish this picture. I am sure I will win the prize. A brand new set of books, with coloured pictures, my heart is beating fast …

Miss Buttigieg is walking around the room. She is approaching my desk. She is just behind me. Her shadow is now darkening my drawing. I can hear the shuffling of the children in their seats. They have finished so much earlier than me that they are getting restless and a little bored.

Miss Buttigieg grabs my picture, holds it up and examines it. I am waiting, my heart beating fast. I am sure she will like it.

Then I see her holding aloft my picture and hear her calling out loudly:

'*This*, boys and girls, is this girl's depiction of *The Princess and the Pea*! A caricature of Her Royal Highness, our dear Princess Elizabeth herself.' I do not understand what she means, but I know she is displeased, angry at me. All the anticipation and excitement turns to dread. I am quaking in my shoes. I feel as if I am about to wet my pants, but control myself.

She continues, and in the meantime a hundred pairs of eyes are on me. 'Don't you ever listen to the broadcasts? Didn't you know you have to learn the stories of Hans Christian Andersen? What have you been doing all these weeks?'

I cannot tell her what I have been doing all these last weeks when I am not at school: washing dirty floors, dusting furniture, changing nappies, running errands for us and for the neighbours, feeding the chickens, cleaning the rabbit hutch, while my school friends are listening to the stories on their radio.

'This is what *The Princess and the Pea* looks like!' She holds aloft for me someone's picture of a pale misshapen stick figure of a little girl lying on several mattresses and a pea underneath them all. I am completely stunned by the absurdity of it.

My hopes for winning the prize for my picture are completely shattered as I hear Miss Buttigieg tearing my drawing to shreds. I am crying noiselessly and I am so blinded by tears that I can only hear the swish and rustle of torn parchment in Miss Buttiegieg's large and cruel hands. My red, white and blue picture of the princess and her sweet pea flowers massacred along with any prospect of winning a prize. But worse still, I cry hot tears of humiliation in front of the entire school.

I am relieved, however, that as the headmistress starts to collect the drawings from the rest of the pupils, she forgets about me. She does not beat me on the hands with the big ruler this time, and for that I am grateful.

THE SECRET

THERE IS SOMETHING ABOUT MY mother which is the source of her constant irritation: she has a worm, a *duda*, in her body, a long, long tapeworm made of little pieces which are shed constantly and are continuously replaced. Its head has hooks and suckers by which it attaches itself to the wall of her intestine. Mother has had it for years, through pregnancies and illnesses. She must have got infected by it when she ate salted but uncooked pork, which had been one of the poor people's main sources of nutrition after the war.

We are all in awe of mother, scared of what the *duda* might do to her, and in turn what she might do to us. Every time she goes to the bathroom she gives us a run down, a graphic description of the *duda*. How many segments have been shed, what colour they were. Sometimes she makes us have a look at the contents of the chamber pot.

Every so often mother subjects herself to another medication, most of it quite terrible: large, black, bitter tablets impossible to swallow, or viscous, evil-smelling liquids, which taste of nitric acid. I am frightened that mother will die and the worm would survive.

To be sure that the *duda* is dead, she has to ascertain that its head has been shed, the distinctive ugly head with its satanic hooks and suckers.

Every time a new treatment is prescribed, we are asked to come and have a look at the chamber pot. Horrified, we look down trying to see if the head of the monster is there. This process is repeated, but with no success. The *duda* is invincible, hanging on in my mother's guts, and tormenting us with its presence by shedding bits of itself but never giving up. We detest it. We have private nightmares about it; but we do not talk about it among ourselves, let alone with our friends. It is too horrible. It is our family secret.

In the schoolyard, big Doris Vella corners me and grabs me by my blouse. I have been trying to avoid her by hiding behind pillars or other children. I am frightened of Doris, and though I try to stay calm, my heart is beating so fast, I feel that it is almost going to burst.

'I know why you are away from school so often,' she sneers.

'My mother has …' I am about to blurt out the truth about my mother, but stop myself in time.

'Yes, what does your mother have, Karmelina Borg?'

'Mother has a new baby,' I lie.

The sneer changes to raucous laughter:

'That brother of yours is only a few months old. I know where babies come from and how long it takes to make them, and you don't, ha, ha, ha, Karmelina!'

'That's not true!' I protest. My eyes are hurting from the effort of trying not to cry, not to break down and betray my secret, our family secret, especially to vile Doris Vella.

'Nits and lice, that's what you have, Karmelina, that's why you're away from school so often. Nits and lice,' she yells for the whole world to hear. She pulls my pigtails as hard as she can, and then wipes her hands on my blouse with great disgust.

'Karmelina Borg has nits and lice, lice and nits!' she chants.

From then on, I am shunned by most of my classmates.

In the end mother has had enough: she is sick of the pain, the discomfort, the inconvenience of the tapeworm segments crawling down her leg, the constant scrutiny of the contents of the chamber pot.

Mother gives Doctor Sammut an ultimatum: either he gives her a medication that is capable of dislodging the beast's head from her intestine, something so strong that it will kill it and its repulsive offspring, or she will start bringing her chamber pot and its foul smelling contents to the waiting room in his surgery. The doctor is never in any doubt that mother is as good as her word. She knows that embarrassment is the most potent weapon she can wield against him.

If that happens, our humiliation will be complete.

Dr Sammut prescribes what he claims is the poison to end all poisons. This time mother has to starve for two days: she is to eat or drink nothing: not a crumb or a drop of water is to enter her lips. Then, at the end of this fasting period, she has to drink an entire bottle of a black potion which is so strong, we are told, that if a drop of it falls on the floor, it is capable of carving a hole in the tiles.

Mother stays in bed for these two days of complete fasting while we look after the house and each other as best we can. I have just turned nine, but as I am the oldest girl, it is up to me to take care of the children. I do not go to school for several days, and I know that I have already missed enough days to fall under the jurisdiction of the Truancy Act.

There is a buff envelope we have received. It looks official: with OHMS, On His Majesty's Service, written in large letters on it. It has not been opened, even though the postmark says that it is a few days old. I am the only one who can read in this household, and I can guess that the letter has to do with my frequent absence from school. I do not show it to anybody.

When I summon enough courage, I open it surreptitiously and read it, understanding enough of the words to confirm my fears:

> *The long absence from school of your daughter, Karmelina Borg, without permission, contravenes Section 35 of the Law of Compulsory Education of minors under 11 years of age. It is therefore incumbent upon your self to explain within five days of receiving this warning, the reason for her absenting herself. The penalty for not complying is a FINE of £20 and/or a possible jail sentence for the parent or guardian of the said child.*

The letter is written in English and Maltese. The Maltese version is even more pedantic and threatening. I am really in trouble. I have somehow expected this, although I did not think it would happen to me. But the last thing I want to do is to upset mother in her delicate state, so I tear the letter into tiny pieces and throw them away in the garbage.

In the meantime, there is a feeling of great expectation at home. We are confident that this time Dr Sammut's concoction is going to work. It will probably harm mother more than the *duda*, but it's worth a try. Anything is worth a try.

We watch mother with anxiety as she drinks this dreadful medicine. It is so bitter, so caustic, that after a few teaspoons, mother vomits it all up. We look on, helpless, trying to encourage her to drink the rest of the bottle. This angers her: *I can't drink this poison! It's alright for you, you don't know how terrible it is!*

Mother is crying. We have not seen her crying like this before, she has been weakened by her long fast and now she seems to have lost the desire to get rid of the tapeworm at all costs.

We urge her on, cradle her head, and dilute the mixture with water till she ingests the entire contents of the bottle. We wipe her hot brow with a wet cloth, as we have seen her do to us when we ourselves have a fever.

Exhausted, her face puffed and covered with tears and her long, jet black hair in complete disarray around her, she collapses in a heap. We help her back to bed and try to restore some order in the house. We make sure that the chamber pot is clean and we put it under her bed ready to receive the long awaited *duda's* head.

Hours pass and nothing happens. Mother is wailing and groaning.

We are terrified that she is going to die. And who is going to look after us if she goes? Maybe the neighbours, our aunts and uncles, or nanna would. But they all have their hands full as it is. Maybe we will all be sent to an orphanage. Wait a minute, what about father? We have not seen him for weeks. He is away, eking out a living for us in the salt pans. But how can he look after five children and a baby while working to support us?

Then all of a sudden we hear a cry coming from mother's room. We hold our breath. Something is happening. One way or another there is going to be some outcome to this tense situation.

We tiptoe to the bedroom, full of apprehension and anticipation. There is a most foetid smell emanating from the chamber pot. And yes, triumphantly we point at the hateful and eagerly awaited head, with its long, long segmented body all curled up in a heap.

The brute has been vanquished. It has been expelled. We feel a sense of victory, of triumph and of immense relief. The demon has been exorcised.

The Needlework Teacher

It was obvious the moment our Needlework teacher had walked into our classroom, with her elegant quilted bag, high heels and fishnet stockings, that she was someone who was going to be the butt of our jokes.

Miss Farrugia, we all agreed, was *il-Mewt*, Death, the Grim Reaper. She had cheeks so hollow that she was almost skeletal, hair so fine that her pink scalp showed through her permed curls. She must have been at least as old as our grandmothers. And yet, from the neck down, she was like Gina Lollobrigida, our favourite film star. It was the combination of ugliness and perfection in the same person that knocked us sideways. She was a contradiction we could not handle.

One by one, out of her large bag came the tools of her trade: boxes of needles, thimbles and scissors, coloured marking chalk, books of patterns and graph papers, sheets of brown paper. She put all of these items systematically on her desk, finally placing a Parker pen, some well-sharpened pencils, rubbers, and sticks of blackboard chalk in the appropriate grooves. We watched her, ready to giggle if she dropped any item on the floor. She didn't.

Neither did she waver when, unassisted by rulers, she drew perfect straight lines and right angles on the blackboard without the use of set squares. When she sketched armholes and necklines freehand, they were so precise, we gasped. And when it came to circles—a pair of the most accurate concentric circles for a skirt—she did not use blackboard compasses. She reminded me of Giotto.

At home, I watched my mother, unschooled and illiterate, making her own sewing patterns on rough paper. I had observed her unpicking a garment and using the parts as patterns, so I had a fair idea of what the subject involved. At school with my upper-middle-class friends, I never mentioned my mother's splendid gift with scissors, needle, and sewing machine. To do this, to brag about my clever mother, would have been tantamount to declaring where I really came from—lower-class stock—with a mother whose husband could not support her with the small wage he earned. To put enough food on her family's table, my mother had to sew clothes for others. And I was too proud to expose her as someone who was not much more than a servant, dependent on other people's whims for work, and who paid her only how much, and when, it suited them. One particularly wealthy woman, whose exquisite taste in clothes was only matched by her meanness, would only pay when her sea captain husband came home from his maritime duties, which was not very often.

My ambidextrous mother could sew a man's jacket with all its intricacies of slippery satin linings, innumerable invisible pockets, shoulder padding, and awkward buttons. Of buttonholes themselves—a dead giveaway for the inexperienced—my mother was an expert. I watched her with admiration verging on envy as she put together a lady's tailored jacket made of the softest woollen material. Each panel had to fit together to bring about the bust shape, then the panels would come in at the waist and sit on the hips with a most divine curve. She would sew the entire lining separately and then insert it into the jacket so none of the seams would show when the garment was taken off. I watched her cutting, with a firm hand which rarely hesitated, satin and silk, organdie and organza, expensive materials for which clients paid more per yard than the money she would receive for her toil.

There was one thing we never touched: her scissors. In those post-war days in Malta, when everything was so scarce, to own a really good pair of scissors was rare. If there was a heinous act in our household, it would have been to use mother's scissors to cut paper. Every now and then a man would come with a cart and special tools to sharpen scissors and knives. As we gazed at the sparks flying, mother would watch like a hawk in case it was not done properly. I often worried that her precious pair of scissors would be eroded on the grinding wheel.

Needlework at our very academic school was only a minor subject: once a week at the end of the school day.

My problem with Needlecraft started on the afternoon when Miss Farrugia handed us a small rectangle of the purest white calico to each student. We were supposed to practise doing different types of hem stitches and mitred corners. On my lap, and wedged open under my desk was *Beau Ideal*. When Miss Farrugia was giving instructions, I was at a very exciting part of the book with the mystery of the precious stone about to be revealed. I simply could not contain my curiosity, for, having already read *Beau Geste* and *Beau Sabreur*, I had invested too much time in the characters and the story to pay attention to what had to be done to a mere rectangle of cloth. At home I had seen shantung and crêpe de chine in quantities ample enough to make curtains with. If I were to ruin this small piece of calico, I'd get another one, wouldn't I?

After my hurried attempts at stitching an even hem failed, I did not get another piece of calico. Sorry, that was the ration for the day. There were only as many squares of fabric as there were girls in the class. I had to unpick my stitches and use the same piece of calico—again and again—till both the cloth and the thread turned into a brownish grey hue, as if they had been trodden upon by a muddy shoe. Any starch or stiffening on that memorable rectangle of material was by then quite gone. I saw my classmates holding aloft some immaculate masterpieces with perfectly uniform stitching, while mine was just a limp caricature.

There was never a hair out of place on Miss Farrugia's almost bald head, and I noticed with secret admiration that her skirts were so well cut, so stylish, that even my mother would have been impressed. Her blouses, hand-embroidered and with scalloped collars, were simply beautiful.

'*Il-Mewt* does have nice clothes, doesn't she?' I said to Edith, hoping to get this snobbish girl to be my friend or at least to have a conversation with me.

'Huh,' she replied, 'I would not be seen *dead* wearing something like that! You obviously know nothing about clothes,' she added spitefully.

I controlled my impulse to say something like: 'How many garments has your mother made?' or 'Do you realise how much work there is in what Miss was wearing?' I knew that such a retort from me would have elicited a bigger put down. Edith's mother would not have been seen dead sewing clothes. She would have had her own *hajjata*, her own seamstress, for such menial tasks.

By the next Needlework class I had finished the *Beau* trilogy and was deep into Baroness Orczy's *The Scarlet Pimpernel* series. Miss Farrugia handed out a sheet of paper to each student. The pattern we were to draw was that of a pair of bloomers. Now I had half a mind to take a real interest in this project, seeing that my own underwear had so many patches on it, it was hard to identify their original material. A new pair of bloomers would have been a real bonus, especially made by me rather than by my overworked mother.

But again my addiction to reading adventure books, like a potent drug, took hold of me. Not only did I not listen to the instructions, but leaving everything till the last moment, I produced a garment which was badly cut, wrongly sewn together, and would have gained not more than a one-out-of-ten.

I did not understand the full reality of my failure with this garment until one day our French lesson—a subject I adored and excelled at—was interrupted by Karla Portelli, a very attractive but dumb senior girl who was always running errands for the teachers, probably to avoid doing class work.

Our teacher was a tall, good-looking priest who had studied at the Sorbonne. We all had a crush on him and—being a man among so many women—he was quite fascinating.

'Excuse me Père Rénaud, Miss Farrugia has a very important message for Karmelina Grech,' she said, her long, dark eyelashes fluttering.

Hearing my name uttered in the same sentence as that of my Needlework teacher, I knew that bad news was to follow.

Holding aloft the offensive pair of bloomers I had manufactured a few days before, Karla delivered this message:

'Miss Farrugia said to Karmelina to take these bloomers home, un-pick them, sew them again and bring them for the next class. Also Miss Farrugia wants a written permission from Karmelina's mother so Karmelina can stay after school to do some extra work.'

Not only was the unmentionable object the most embarrassing thing that could have been held up in front of this priest, but my reputation as a brilliant scholar was suddenly and brutally shattered.

There was just a hint of a smile on Père Rénaud's face.

'*Bien, alors, Karmelina, est-ce-que tu as entendu le message de Mademoiselle Farrugia?*' he asked me, in a matter of fact way, as if he were discussing the conjugation of an irregular French verb.

'*Oui, merci, Père Rénaud,*' I said, snatching the garment from Karla's hand and stuffing it in my desk. My face was burning, and from the corner of my eyes I could see the rest of the class nudging each other and trying to suppress their giggles.

There was little chance that I could have followed Miss Farrugia's instructions. Firstly, I did not want to incur mother's anger, and besides, mother could neither read nor write. So I hatched a plot which I hoped would save my skin.

In our village lived a very prosperous couple whose only child, Marie, went to a private school, but I had learnt through gossip that she was a bit slow. I also knew that at her school they did Needlecraft as a 'proper' subject and that she made the most marvellous costumes. Marie and I had been in Catechism class together and I had often seen her in church with her besotted parents, all very smartly dressed. They always stopped to ask about my studies as I was the first girl in the street to pass the entrance exam for Secondary School.

I struck a deal with Marie. I would help her with her algebra—more like do it for her, as it turned out—and she would fix my bloomers and do my needlework homework.

The matter of the note to Miss Farrugia was less complicated. With a different handwriting to mine, I wrote a grovelling letter saying how sorry I was to have a daughter who did not listen to instructions.

Dear Miss Farrugia, It is with the greatest regret that I learnt that my daughter, Karmelina Grech, has been showing insubordination

and disrespect towards someone as kind and hard working as your-
self, and that, through her thoughtlessness she has brought shame on
our family. I was quite shocked when she told me about her inex-
cusable behaviour, because at home she is a veritable angel, indeed,
because of my infirm condition and crippling disease she is more
like my right hand. I would humbly ask you to punish her, not by
detention, which unfortunately would punish me indirectly, but by
giving her some really long essay to complete at home …

A detention would have alerted my strict mother to my bad
behaviour, whereas a long essay, written at home under her illiterate
eyes, would pass unnoticed.

It worked! I could see that Miss Farrugia was impressed with the
note:

'Your poor mother! She must be a very nice person.' I almost
replied:

'You don't live with her, like I do!' But instead, I smiled sweetly,
happy that my note was believed. Miss Farrugia was absolutely thrilled
with my re-done bloomers. Marie had sewn the most perfect stitches
and had trimmed all the frayed edges. She, or really her maid, had
even washed, starched and ironed the garment for me.

Once a week I'd go and look at her atrocious algebra notebook, and
help her with the work, which I enjoyed, as it was also an excuse for
me to avoid housework.

'But what is x, Karmelina?' she used to ask, wringing her hands
with anguish at her lack of understanding of the subject.

'Anything you like' I kept telling her. 'It changes all the time,
depending on what the problem is!'

I liked Marie a lot, she had none of the airs and graces of some
of the *nouveaux riches* that the war had produced. Also her mother

always gave me two pieces of cake, one for me and one to take home.

I began to notice that Miss Farrugia's hands were becoming shaky and her fingers more gnarled. Her blackboard lines and circles were becoming more uneven and she always sat down after explaining a task, something she hardly ever did before. Her voice became squeaky, she was often breathless, and she started to use a walking stick. Somehow, we were a little sorry for her and stopped our silly giggling. We began to pay more attention in her class.

One day after term holidays, our headmistress, wearing a solemn face, came to our class. 'I'm afraid I have some very bad news, girls.' Her voice wavered and she had to clear her throat and fight back tears. 'Miss Farrugia, your Needlework teacher, has left us. She passed away a few days ago. As you may have noticed, she had a degenerative disease which was incurable and which had made her appear so much older than she really was. She was only thirty five.'

FUCHSIAS

I WAS BORN IN MALTA during the war, during a raid by the enemy planes. Now one thing my late mother never told me was whether I was born before or after she was abandoned by the nurses and the doctor—they all ran down to the bomb shelter and left her alone. Mother held such hatred for hospitals in general that she later insisted on giving birth to her other seven children at home with the local midwife assisting. She also refused to ever spend a night in a hospital for the rest of her life.

The neighbourhood of my childhood was an extension of my family. For me it was a crescent-shaped row of houses off the main street. This was where I learnt about life and death, and where my most impressionable years were spent. Prominent above everybody else was Sylvia—smart, fair-haired Sylvia, confident, superior, knowledgeable. Then there was Fredu, her younger brother, the bane of our lives, the breaker of our games, the cross we had to bear. There were other boys and girls in the neighbourhood, but Sylvia and Fredu were special: their father had gone to Australia and when he sent them letters, infrequently, we would all assemble around them in awe. Those filmy thin blue papers, those letters written in ungrammatical Maltese, had traversed the earth. Those picture-books, so rare and precious in our post-war existence among the rubble of the war, held us spellbound. We imagined that the hands which sent those letters could well have touched a kangaroo or a koala, or a platypus even, mythical objects, beasts of wonder!

What, to an outsider, must have appeared as an arid and joyless environment, was to us a place full of magical things to play with, climb, hide in and paint. A Moreton Bay fig in a nearby public garden, was a source of great enjoyment for us, its small firm fruits were used as spinning tops called *cuppitati*. Those who could make their tops spin longest became the champions of the neighbourhood.

A gigantic and gnarled carob tree, with branches tortured by winds of a thousand winters and twisted crazily in all directions, made an excellent hiding place for us. Often, we would make a hammock or a swing to provide endless fun as we hung among the leathery leaves, chewing the sweet brown pods, our substitute for chocolates. Chocolates were things we only saw in the shops in the city, and we rarely tasted them.

Once, I had arranged to meet Sylvia beside the carob tree. I had planned to blurt out my passionate love for her. I hid among the boughs and waited for what appeared to be an eternity. When I saw her coming along, chaperoned by Fredu, like a coward I ran away. She did not see me and, thinking that I had jilted her, for a long time treated me like her enemy.

In their game the girls used glass beads, which they flicked from a line, drawn on the ground, into a little hole. Each coloured bead was worth a certain number of points, and red was the most valuable. I remember my sisters taking their red beads everywhere with them, including hiding them in their pillows so as not to lose them. The person who scored the most points with the least number of shots won the game. Boys played a similar game but with large marbles. How I loved to roll those coloured glass spheres in the sunlight to catch the images around me, like a magic convex eye.

At times we used soft pieces of limestone discarded from building sites, and we would carve them into miniature houses, complete with balconies and windows. Or we would carve a church, with colonnades and cupolas, and wide staircases leading to its portals. We squeezed berries, leaves and petals to make a brew and used it to paint our sculptures, keeping each combination of colours a secret from our mates.

No piece of cloth or cotton thread from a tailor or dressmaker was ever wasted, as the girls would turn it into dolls' clothes, tiny curtains, little bags; and the tiny left-over pieces from their creations would be used to stuff pillows, or soft toys, cushions or dolls' mattresses. Scraps of wood from the carpenter were made into toy carts, or other toy furniture. My sisters were lucky enough to have a wooden doll's pram, with a rounded hood made of cane.

Two empty tins of shoe polish and a bit of string made a perfect set of weighing scales for us to play 'shopkeepers', with buttons, beads and marbles used instead of weights. 'Could I have 5 beads of pumpkin and 3 buttons of potatoes please?'

We raided our parents' kitchens for merchandise, which we chopped up and distributed in tiny containers. Sometimes there was no food at all, but undeterred, we would use small pieces of gravel picked from the ruins around us.

On windy days, we flew kites from the flat roofs and the sky would be filled with festive colours swaying and flapping, swooping and rising, soaring, and sometimes getting caught up in a playful tangle with each other, against a background of heavenly cloudlessness.

Some Sundays were delightfully special. We would go and stay with grandma, at the edge of the village. In the foyer of her house there was a large and lush fuchsia plant in a hanging basket. It was the only fuchsia in the village and it was something we gazed at in wonder but were never allowed to touch. The pendulous pink and purple flowers were called *imsielet* or earrings, and were a source of fascination to visitors. Nanna's fuchsia was famous in the whole village. People came from the other end of the village just to see this amazing plant.

Our grandparents' house, which was surrounded by productive fields, was so much more fun. Nanna would prepare a piece of lamb, killed by grandpa the previous day. This was a process kept strictly away from the children's eyes, lest we'd practise the same methods on our younger brothers and sisters, or so it was feared!

Nanna placed the meat in a large baking dish with potatoes and onions freshly dug from the brown lumpy soil that morning, and sprinkled liberally with fresh herbs and with dried aromatic seeds, caraway and sesame, from the sweet-smelling earthenware jars in her kitchen, stored away from the bright sunlight. Then it would be ready for its journey to the baker's oven.

I remember going to the baker with my grandma to the joyful ringing of church bells, and to the music of guitars in the village bars. Odours of baked chicken, turkey, meat, cakes and bread, would surge forward to greet me. Fascinated by the fabulous tongues of fire, I watched as the baker and his rotund wife stirred the ashes to make miniature fireworks inside the oven. Nanna's eyesight was failing, so I had to make sure that the number on the metal 'ticket' was the same as the one put in our baking dish. At midday, with the Angelus bells pealing a full festive volley, we would all file up to claim our baked dinner, meat brown and shiny, steaming hot and with the piquant smell of the caraway on the potatoes.

I close my eyes now, and I can still smell, feel and hear that childhood scene.

Nannu Pitru was a quiet man who never uttered a word while we ate. Besides, he never had a chance, since Nanna was a woman who never stopped talking and asking us questions.

Now something about adults that really used to get me was their knowledge about everything, and their certitude about the world around them. I, being always full of doubts and racked with uncertainty, perhaps because of my shaky entrance into the world, envied this state, and longed to grow up to be like them. When I was in secondary school we studied 'The Island Continent of Australia', being another pink country on the world map like Malta and the other British Commonwealth countries. To the question 'How many merino sheep are there in Australia?' the answer which I was meant to give in the exam was 75 million. But I also added 'give or take a few hundred', which gave me a nought for that answer.

The other question I came to grief on, was the one about the length of the Murray-Darling river system and its tributaries. The text book and my geography teacher knew exactly how long that system was, but my doubts started to show on paper. What happened when there is a flood, or a drought? There was no such agonising on my teacher's part. She looked me straight in the eye, adjusted the pink mohair cardigan on her ample bosom, and said, 'That's how long it is, Albert Zammit, and that's that, full stop.'

It was about this time that my heart was nearly broken because Sylvia and her family left Malta to join their father in Australia. I secretly started writing to Sylvia using the address of a friend whose mother was very liberal and did not mind the correspondence. Only, I hated the way he always read her return letters before I did!

How I had envied her as we saw them go off on the *Sydney* from the Grand Harbour. Her father was then working in the power station at Yallourn. At first she wrote profusely about the country, about floods and bush fires, and I so longed to be there on some wild expedition, saving her from roaring waters or raging fires. Sylvia wrote about thunderstorms and cyclones which did not seem to affect her at all, because she absolutely loved the place.

One of her letters was especially memorable: *You know there was a big fuchsia plant in our garden, like the one your Nanna had in her house. Only this one was big, as big as a bush. Dad cut it down to plant potatoes! I was a bit sad to see it thrown away …*

How I yearned to be old enough to go there and elope with her! How I suffered each Christmas, thinking about her, imagining her on some golden beach in Gippsland. And in summer, how tormented I was every time the song about a polka dot bikini came over the radio, and how strange it all sounded when the warning that the wearing of bikinis on this beach will incur a fine greeted me from large and threatening placards on every beach on the Island.

When I was 19 years of age, I decided that I had had enough, so I put my name down on the long list of prospective migrants for Australia. I had wanted to surprise Sylvia, but when I arrived in Yallourn, it was too late. She was already married! I felt cheated and betrayed, and so I left for Melbourne.

THE VASE

ON MY FIRST ENCOUNTER WITH the vase I was quite enchanted. I could not understand how glass, usually so flat and colourless, could also be so rotund, and come in such captivating hues. I also noted that on the base of this vase there was a tiny indent in the shape of a bird in flight—a tiny carving, as if the maker had tried to leave a secret signature. But when I mentioned this bird to those around me, no one could see anything.

What intrigued me most were the pleated sides of the vase and the fluted rim. And as for those bewitching tints of aquamarine, I had no adequate way to describe them till much later, when the Professor of Physics went into a sort of ecstasy about refraction of light and prismatic surfaces. As a child swimming in the Mediterranean Sea, I used to be surrounded by similar turquoise tints and crystalline blues which defied description.

At that time, I could barely reach the top of the table on which the vase rested, and though I was already five years old, I was so tiny that adults still thought of me as merely a baby. I noticed that adults would talk to each other in front of me about topics they would never dream of broaching in front of other children. It was as if by being so undersized, they assumed my grasp of the world around me was also diminutive, that I could not possibly comprehend what they were saying.

So I learnt some wonderful things, and some terrible things. I became aware that the vase was an object of loathing by everyone else, and that nobody wanted it in their house for long.

'Don't touch that vase, Angelina,' my mother yelled at me, 'and stop staring at it! We're going to wrap it up and give it to Auntie Barbara.'

I had gathered from the whispered conversations around me that Auntie Barbara had done something terrible. At first I did not know what it was she had done to bring down on her the bad feelings of the family.

Then when the grownups were carrying on their gossip session, I played on the floor, rolling my glass beads under their feet. I realised that Auntie Barbara was living with a much older man, who had finally decided to marry her. It seemed that the best way the family would show their feelings of disapproval was to give her the hated vase.

I had been observing, too, that under her voluminous skirts, so fashionable at the time, Auntie Barbara had a bulge on her stomach which later on turned out to be a most beautiful, golden-haired baby boy.

Her husband died soon after they got married, and Auntie introduced *gardiniera* to the village and she became very rich. Auntie could turn anything into *gardiniera*: cabbages, carrots, and even kohl rabi. Always, there were queues of people waiting outside her shop. Even in the searing heat of midday, when the asphalt roads were melting, Auntie Barbara was still chopping vegetables and decanting and plugging large bottles with corks bigger than my head. (I was warned not to lean onto those open bottles or I could drown and die a vinegary death!)

All along I had wondered what had happened to the vase. Auntie's house had become a pickling factory, and any niceties of ornate sideboards or brocaded sofas or cabinets with crystal glassware had been completely dispensed with.

Once, when I washed her floors (and the stench nearly killed me) I discovered a large ceramic chamber pot filled with fat gold sovereigns under the matrimonial bed. After that, while Auntie was busy in the shop, and the baby was asleep, I would take out the coins and play with them. I loved the way I could roll them along the terrazzo floor. And I adored the way the rays of sunlight made the stern woman, who I knew was Queen Victoria, *Regina Imperatrix*, blink, as she came out of darkness into the dazzling light. I was a very efficient worker and gave the coins an extra polish before returning them to the gigantic pot.

Then, one day, I opened a door in the wall and there was the vase! I nearly hugged it. But away from the light, it looked sad and aloof. I caressed its undulating sides and ran my fingers on the tiny bird etched on its base. Everything in my world was rough and unattractive, but here I had the gentle vase all to myself!

The next time I saw the vase, out in the open, was when ousin Peppi married his childhood sweetheart, Rozanna. Auntie Barbara, who was too busy making *gardiniera*, did not have time to go out looking for a present, so naturally she gave them the vase as a wedding gift.

By then I had grown a few inches taller, and it was very economical for Peppi and Rozanna to have me as their bridesmaid, because I had just done my first Holy Communion and already owned a white dress. Unfortunately, I had just lost my front teeth, so I was severely warned not to smile during the photo session, or I would spoil the bridal picture.

My reputation as a brilliant washer of terrazzo floors had spread like wildfire among the relatives, and I was back on hands and knees this time for Rozanna, who was looking like a sail in full wind. Only, Rozanna's floors were a pleasure to clean, and did not smell of rotting *gardiniera*.

One day, Rozanna's sister, Anna, sent a letter from Melbourne. And what I read on the filmy blue paper broke my heart.

Dearest Rozanna, I hope you are not feeling too ill with the baby. We are living with Joe's parents in Sunshine, and I don't like it at all. You know the blue vase you gave us as a farewell present? It arrived safely, wrapped in a blanket. I was very upset, however, by the howls of laughter from Joe's mother when she saw the other things I brought from Malta: the washing soda, the kerosene lamps, the candles, the methylated spirits stove. She not only killed herself laughing at us, but she also brought some neighbours who fell over with amusement at the sight of those objects. I am still so embarrassed that I have hardly spoken to anybody …

So THE VASE, MY BEAUTIFUL blue friend and the little bird, were on the other side of the earth!

At times I was tempted to believe that it would break and be thrown in some municipal tip: an inglorious burial among rotting vegetation, dead cats and corroded bed springs. But I knew that an object like that would not die easily.

When I migrated to Australia, I tried desperately to locate the vase.

'Oh, we didn't keep that ghastly object long, we donated it to the white elephant stall at the fête,' Anna told me. 'God knows who bought it! Such a hideous thing, don't you reckon? We were burgled once, and everything that was not nailed to the ground was stolen from our lounge room, except that vase. Just as well, because we used to save our money underneath the plastic flowers!'

Heartbroken, I kept looking for the vase among bric à brac stalls in markets, antique and secondhand shops.

Then one day I spotted it in an Auction of Antiques! The vase in the glass cabinet was the same vase which had cast its spell on me so long ago. The azure colours and the wavy rim were there and, when I looked closely, I could see the little bird imprint on its base. There could only be one vase like that in the entire world.

A gold-edged card declared its Provenance:

Circa 1798. Murano, Italy. Disappeared during the French Revolution. Reappeared around 1899 in England, where it spent last 100 years at Barrington Manor.

'That's absolute garbage!' I shouted at the auctioneer. 'That vase has spent many years in Malta moving from one relative of mine to another. Barrington Manor, my foot! It's more like Auntie Barbara's smelly *gardiniera* shop, and then in Sunshine, holding a bunch of plastic flowers. That vase sir,' I said, most emphatically, pointing to the highlight of the auction, 'has crossed the Equator wrapped in a blanket inside a tea chest among several articles which my relatives believed would make tolerable their first years in this country, as it was presumed that while the streets were paved with gold, and teeming with kangaroos, there were no such things as soap and lamps and stoves.'

'Madam,' he replied, 'please leave the premises or I'll call the police.'

On auction day, I watched the bidding on the vase rise to some enormous figure, well beyond my means. My dark glasses hid the tears of sadness and joy, for now at last my beloved vase was going to be delivered to a good home.

2

Melbourne

Folds of Fat

Lisa came to my bedroom one night when the window panes were fogged over, the outside temperature close to zero. She said that she could not keep warm in her bed, and that she had been unable to sleep with loneliness since her boyfriend had left.

'You are very kind, Sylvia, I don't know how to say thank you enough,' she told me.

'Don't say anything, just try to sleep.'

God knows I myself needed sleep. Four lectures before lunch tomorrow, three hours of prac in the afternoon. Lisa's day did not start till after lunch so she could afford to sleep in and still get to all her lectures.

I didn't know how I was supposed to rest with her—a bag of bones, her flannelette pajamas much too big for her—in my single bed. I made room for her, hoping that her sharp bony hips wouldn't come too close. At least her teeth had stopped chattering now and her wizened face looked calmer than when she had knocked on my bedroom door asking to be let in. I must not have sounded too kind, in spite of what she had said, because she stopped talking, rolled over on her side and using the pillow and the blankets she had brought with her, made as if to fall asleep.

I noticed that she had bald pink patches on her scalp: maybe the reason for those pert little berets she always wore even inside the house.

An hour or so later, I was woken up from a deep sleep and a feeling of having been interrupted in the middle of a pleasant dream. Lisa had pulled all the bedclothes on to her side and was moaning and twisting and turning.

'For God's sake, Lisa,' I said, and though loud enough to wake her up, she did not reply. 'I need my bloody sleep, and there's only a couple of hours before I have to get up!' I told her, pulling back my blankets onto my side of the bed.

I HAD MOVED IN WITH Lisa a few weeks before; her previous flatmate had gone and she needed someone to share the rent, while I wanted to be within walking distance of the university. The rent was cheap, Lisa was very quiet and hardly ever came into our shared kitchen. The only reason I knew she was in her room was because she'd be playing, over and over, the Dave Brubeck quartet's 'Take five' and 'Pick up sticks', the saxophone's plangent sound piercing our lonely spaces. I didn't mind, I could not afford a radio, let alone a record player, and I found the music soothing, if a little repetitive.

Just as well she was not interested in cooking, because only one gas burner worked and the oven was dangerous to use, the landlord had told me—it would start leaking gas if we turned it on. But as I did not have time or money to make any roast dinners or fancy meals, this did not bother me at all.

One thing that had me puzzled, though, was that I had never seen Lisa put anything in her mouth in the way of food. I suspected that she had her meals in the Student Union caf, or at Genevieve's in Carlton where the intelligentsia—or those who pretended—met for lively conversations. My budget did not stretch to eating out, and my weekend job of waitressing in a city café was barely sufficient to keep my rent and expenses covered.

Lisa's parents, she had told me, lived in Brighton and were very well off. She had given me a glimpse of her wardrobe once and I could see some beautiful thick woollen jumpers, tartan skirts, tailored coats, fur-lined boots and gloves, all so much superior to my own clothes. In fact Lisa had told me that I could borrow anything from her if I wanted— only I was too shy to take up the offer. Besides, I had nothing good enough to match those garments, and she was so much slimmer.

One day I quizzed Lisa about her eating, and to my amazement she replied, 'Folds of fat, Sylvia, huge folds of fat!' and as she said so, she pinched her tummy, as if to show me a spare tyre of blubber, but which was, in fact, several layers of clothes she wore to keep herself warm.

I managed to get a few hours of fitful rest while Lisa whimpered and muttered as if she was having a bad dream. I was certain that, by lunchtime, I would be so tired that I'd fall asleep on my desk. But there was no point in staying in bed, so I decided to go to the kitchen to make myself a cup of tea.

In the dark, narrow corridor, where the stale odours of the downstairs tenants' cooking still hovered, I had to be careful not to trip on the torn linoleum. The air in our dimly lit kitchen was even colder than in our decrepit and inefficient fridge, and I wrapped my dressing gown tightly around me.

I had been looking forward to some peanut butter on my toast—peanut butter being one of the products the New World had introduced me to, and I liked it. But, to my annoyance, the jar was completely empty.

'Bloody hell!' I yelled to the empty kitchen. 'That jar was almost full when I last used it!' Bloody Lisa must have eaten it all, no wonder she couldn't sleep.

My first impulse was to go back to the bedroom, wake her up and shake her—make her apologise for devouring my peanut butter.

But I took a deep breath and stopped myself. How could I do that to an already tormented creature?

Looking through the dusty, curtainless sash window towards the sun rising on a bright new day, I could see the roofs of the neighbouring houses: the frost thawing and steaming, the patterns of moisture on the corrugated iron changing and evaporating as quickly as they were formed, and the moss on the slate tiles shiny in the morning sunlight. It was the first time I had looked from this second-storey level onto those houses, so busy I had been, studying, going to lectures and working. There were times when I had been so tired that I had gone to bed wearing the same clothes I came in from outside with, only to get up in the morning feeling horribly grubby and tired.

My attention was then captured by a nearby backyard. The first impression was one of untidiness—leaning fences, clutter of rusty objects and old wooden boxes. But on closer scrutiny, I could see a large fig tree in its unmistakable winter nakedness. There were several prickly pear bushes—survivors of the inquisition by that voracious foreign beetle introduced for their destruction. There were olive trees, orange, lemon and lime trees, all so stridently southern European, they nearly brought tears of nostalgia to my eyes. A grapevine, bare and gnarled, formed a kind of incomplete ceiling over a verandah full of pots of red geraniums. Near one wall, there were chook pens and rabbit hutches, covered by an abundant morning glory whose blue flowers were beginning to unfurl in the dawn's dew.

A stab of longing for my grandmother's garden in Malta assailed me momentarily. Here the trees were bare, over there her garden would be at its summery best, I reminded myself.

I had been avoiding all possible occasions of homesickness. I had been working in almost a frenzy to eradicate any feelings of regret for coming to Australia without my family. I had tried to avoid any negative comments about this country.

But it was the memory of my grandmother's garden with its profusion of roses, aromatic herbs, dozens of citrus trees, grapes, almonds, vegetables, and the pungent perfume of lavender in her linen cupboard that really hurt. *She* did not have folds of fat, and her soft but compact little body had worked from sunrise to sunset in the fields, to help feed several mouths.

It was moments like these that I had steeled myself against: *don't brood, don't harbour regrets, don't look back.*

Don't look back! I had told myself, not so long before, as I ascended the steps into the Qantas Super Constellation plane—for a trip that would take, in those days, almost a week. Below me, a sea of faces, tearful, sad, were wishing me goodbye at Luqa airport. *Why are they crying? I am going on the adventure of a lifetime. I will be crossing the equator, seeing distant lands, mythical animals, different people.*

My knowledge had been of wide open spaces, merino sheep, artesian wells, gold ingots and soft furry animals. I had not known about inner suburban Melbourne, with its foundries, its decaying shops, its traffic noises, its smells of factories and industrial chemicals.

Now, my earlier violent reaction to the consumed peanut butter appeared to me quite childish and exaggerated, especially if it was emaciated Lisa who had been the culprit. Lisa, gentle, fragile Lisa, starving herself in this country of abundance, seeing folds of fat where there was only skin and bone. Almost bald at twenty, and with the shuffle and bearing of an old woman.

No, I will not go and disturb her rest. Maybe I will not even mention the peanut butter … Maybe soon we can have a hearty meal together and I'll tell her about my grandma's garden …

Such wild beauty that was unfolding right there below me, in this old, scruffy suburb, a little corner of a distant world that was so much like Malta. The consolation that the dark days of winter were on the wane—and that the solstice had come and gone several weeks before—lifted my spirits. I had discovered an island of precious peace in a sea of clamour. I had to relish it before the din of traffic would destroy it. I decided to watch the progress of that garden from our kitchen window, perhaps even get acquainted with the owners …

My cup of tea was now cold. I ate the dry toast and mentally braced myself for the long hard day ahead of me.

The Cardinal Bird

On the twenty-second day of November 1963, a cataclysmic event occurred in the Attard household in Brunswick. I know exactly what we were doing on that day: we were watching the assassination of President John F Kennedy on a 15-inch black-and-white TV screen.

Peppi Attard's entire collection of birds was dead. Every single bird, every finch and chaffinch, male, female, old, young, priceless or common, was found dead in the aviary that eventful morning. When Peppi, an unassuming man who had more knowledge of birds than any zoology professor, came home from his night shift and went to feed his beloved birds, he found them belly up, stiff as boards, dead as doornails, many on the floor of the cage, some on their perch.

His precious collection, his whole life's work, had been destroyed overnight. There was no apparent cause for this catastrophe. There was no sign of forced entry by some wily fox—the wire netting around the cages was intact. The latches were shut. There was no blood on the ground, no sign of a struggle, the aviary floor was not paved with feathers.

Not one was spared. Pert little Doris, aggressive Fredu, happy

Dolor, moody Mina, jolly Jack—all had gone to meet their Maker. Peppi was devastated.

The children were at school, Rita, his wife, was at the factory. He was alone to cope with this tragedy.

I was boarding with the Attards. When I got home from the University, I found the family desolate, utterly inconsolable.

The television, full of nothing else but the Kennedy assassination, was turned on, as it must have been in every single household in the country, if not the entire world. Everybody wanted to know more and more about how a popular young president was shot, in front of a crowd of adoring subjects.

The Attards were shedding an ocean of tears. Were they crying for the President or for their birds?

'We spent so much money on them. We'll never be able to afford them again!'

'What are we to do without the President?'

'Oh poor little Teresa, such a sweet singing voice!'

'Poor Mrs Kennedy, and little John John, imagine how sad it is for them!'

'I spent a fortune on those birds!'

'Why don't you report it to the police?' Mrs Attard pleaded with her husband.

'You know why. And don't ask me again. I wasn't supposed to have so many birds in our backyard. But I have a fair idea who it could have been. I'll fix him!'

At this Mrs Attard burst into another fit of uncontrollable crying.

'You'll go to prison! That's all we need! First the birds, then the President. If you go to prison, who's going to support us?'

'Mummy, is Dad going to prison near Nanna's house in Coburg?'

'Don't be silly! Dad is just saying something stupid.'

'I'll tell you who's bloody stupid, Rita. That bastard who poisoned my birds.'

'Don't swear in front of the children, you know how they repeat everything. What will Father Calleja think if he heard them swearing?'

'I couldn't give a bugger what Father Calleja thinks. He hasn't had his entire collection of birds destroyed, has he?'

'Does Father Calleja have an aviary too, Dad?'

I just sat and listened. In light of the tragedy, I felt hopelessly inadequate to offer any consolation. So I said nothing.

THAT NIGHT I HAD A memorable dream. I dreamt that a huge flock of birds was circling in the sky above my head. What was so striking about them was their brilliance. Their colours were luminescent, dazzling, intense. Purple martins with their velvety blues; Baltimore orioles with their orange breasts; yellow warblers the colour of sunflowers; cockatoos pink as if freshly painted with duco, quails with patterns which seemed sprayed on by a mad graffiti artist.

The spaces between their feathers splitting the light like a refracting lens, each bird looked like the descent of the Holy Spirit, with a celestial rainbow springing from outstretched wings. A Pentecost of polycoloured avian paracletes.

In the centre of this flock, leading it, there was a splendid cardinal bird, its feathers the most dazzling red silk.

To my horror the bird was flying straight at me.

'I told you not to leave your native country,' said the cardinal bird. It had my mother's stern voice, her penetrating eyes.

'But you are in Malta, Mother, how come you're here in Brunswick as well?'

She gave me a fierce look at this stupid question, but continued in her severe voice:

'You have defied my orders, you have gone to the other side of the earth, where danger lurks everywhere, venomous creatures at every turn.'

'But, mother, I'm in Brunswick here. The only danger is from Sydney Road traffic.'

'Do not answer back, child. Just contemplate the misery you have caused us.'

'But mother, I've been a very good girl, studying, doing my assignments …'

She continued, as if she hadn't heard what I said.

'Do you realise the dishonour you have inflicted on the family?' her dark eyes penetrating mine.

'I'm sorry, Mother, I thought you'd be proud of me, coming here on my own …'

'Proud!' she squawked, the sound echoing in the void around her, the other birds having disappeared. She hovered menacingly against a cloudless sky. 'Proud, indeed! Do you realise that only the illiterate, the unemployable and the hopeless migrate?'

'That's nonsense!'

'You don't have to live with the hurtful comments I get everyday, that's why.'

'But I'm happy here in Brunswick, Mother! There's everything I need on Sydney Road, and other things that I don't need, like banjo, mandolin and guitar teachers in the barber's shop. There's a tattooist and a fortune teller, there's an Indian sari shop. What more could the heart desire? Anyway, I have a Chemistry exam tomorrow and I have to study.'

'You left it too late, as always. Always leaving the study to the eve of the exam!' She chided me, the red tuft on her head shaking in disapproval.

'I did not know you were a cardinal, Mother!' I said to mollify her by appealing to her sense of pride and to change the subject.

My ploy worked! She smiled, and above her black bib I could see a tremor of feathery pleasure.

'I am, in fact, the Pope! Haven't you been watching the white smoke in the chimney?'

'Oh, the chimney of the foundry next door? It only belches orange smoke and ruins my underwear.'

'You are so very unobservant, head in air, nose in books, up to no good. You will not be rich at the rate you're going. You are a bitter disappointment to me and to your family.'

'OK then, Mother, if you're so clever, so powerful as to be a pope, how about telling me the questions on the Chemistry exam?'

'I can't. Not directly. It wouldn't be fair on the others.'

'Please Mother, I promise, I'll come back home to Malta when all this is over.'

'You haven't changed: plead, plead, plead, and you get what you want. I should never have signed your migration papers.'

'But, Mum, you didn't. Remember? I forged your signature. Besides, you could only put a cross in the space provided.'

'Insolent girl. Notwithstanding, I will give you a clue for tomorrow's exam. *Chapters 37 to 55.*'

THE NEXT MORNING I GOT UP with a splitting headache. I had no time for the Attards' grief for their dead birds, and though the assassination of a President was very sad, it was too far away. My immediate concern was the exam for which I was ill prepared.

The dream about a cardinal bird had really affected me.

Chapters 37 to 55.

The textbook only had 36 chapters.

SITTING PRETTY

'You know, Gulja, once you get that piece of paper, you'll be sitting pretty.'

The piece of paper Jack McAll was referring to was the degree I was hoping to get at the end of that year. Jack's daughter, Sheila had invited me to spend the last few weeks before the exams at her house in Toorak. I had no family in Australia then, so this seemed to me a wonderful way to avoid the loneliness before the ordeal of the final examinations.

I began to realise that *sitting pretty* was Jack's favourite expression.

'I reckon when we clinch that deal, we'll be sitting pretty,' he said a few times during dinner. Wendy McAll was utterly bored by anything that did not have something to do with fashion, or high society, and intimated that she was not interested. The Melbourne Spring racing carnival was on at the time, and the style of costumes was her all-consuming preoccupation.

She hated the way Jack carried on about him or anybody else *sitting pretty*. She had enough on her hands with Sheila struggling with her law degree without Jack carrying on with his silly jokes and remarks.

This was her fourth year at uni, but her second year studying law.

'Do you know where stockbrokers get their name?' said Jack one day, during one of his jokes.

'No, Jack, we don't know, and we couldn't give a bugger.'

To my dismay, Sheila said, 'Oh mother, please!'

I was embarrassed by his wife's brusque response, and expected some kind of angry retort from Jack. Instead he turned to me and said, 'What about you, Gulja, what do you think?'

'Is it because they break the rules?'

'No sorry, that's not it.'

'I know,' intercepted Sheila, 'it's because it breaks your heart to see the money they get.'

'No, not that either.'

'I honestly don't even know what stockbrokers do. I give up.' This must be some trick question, I thought.

'You're at university and you give up so easily. Well, I'll tell you myself, even though I've only been through the uni on a bicycle.'

This seemed to be one of Jack's jokes about himself. Ever the humble man, he had this thing about not having had a good education, but somehow *managed*. Managed was hardly the word, he was a multi-millionaire with a string of hardware stores around the country.

'Oh no, Dad, what about the times you drove me through uni in the Bentley?'

'Yes, but I'm too long in the tooth to be taken for a student, Sheil.' I could see that these two people liked each other a lot.

'Anyhow, he's called a broker because someone will always end up being broke after having dealt with him.'

'Oh Dad! That's as weak as ditch water.' She said, but still laughing at the joke.

Sheila was a sweet girl, very much like her father, it seemed to me. Her absentmindedness was legendary. On her way to and from school she had been known to tie her books and satchel to her waist, because she was tired of losing things on the tram. At that moment she was trying to grapple with *The Law of Torts*, and using all kinds of weird ways and mnemonics to remember facts, with some success. *Smith versus Cruikshank, Craven versus The Commonwealth Government ... Smith caught the crook by the shank and cowardly Craven copped it from the Crown ...*

Their house was designed so the garden was visible from every part of it. Emilio, the gardener, was obsessive about neatness and ymmetry, a gardener after Wendy McAll's heart. Emilio was expert with topiaries and parterres, and passionate about perfection in privet hedges. He was the only gardener I know who carried a spirit level among his secateurs and snail poisons. The hedges had to be just right: the parallel and perpendicular were not concepts Emilio would joke about. His globular topiaries were so perfectly spherical, Giotto himself would have been quite impressed.

Yet Mrs McAll was never satisfied. A few leaves blown over from next door threw her into a fit of annoyance and they would have to be instantaneously swept away. Nothing was allowed to spoil the neatness of the garden for too long. Mrs McAll had bought a special lawn vacuum cleaner from America. This was an essential part of her armoury against untidiness, and its din was often heard disrupting the tranquillity of the place.

I thought of the scruffy garden in my rented house in Brunswick, with its profusion of weeds mingled with multicoloured lantanas, straggly fuchsias, gaudy marguerite daisies, and dozens of oregano plants reminiscent of its Italian owners. Thank goodness Mrs McAll never visited me, because she would certainly have had heart failure.

That year washed over me like a tide on a craggy shore. I was the recipient of such a great deal of knowledge, of multitudinous facts, and like the inter-tidal creatures on the beach, I had thrived on it. Of the sheer number of names, chemical reactions, laws of physics and of biochemistry, some of the knowledge did incorporate itself into the cells of my brain.

THE PERIMETER THAT BORDERED MY existence was the brown Zoology school, the strident student union with its untidy but lively cafeteria, and the austere ivy clad building of the Botany department. I loved the axolotl in the aquarium at the entrance of the Zoology school, and although this bestowed an air of friendly old-fashioned decay on the building, there were scientists nearby who were doing the very latest in research work. For me the place was a cocoon of security, of orderliness of timetables and schedules, and of quiet erudition which I found most engaging.

Occasionally I strayed into the Beaurepaire building to have a swim between lectures, an activity often cut short by an instructor with a loud hailer who would demand that we clear the pool for the Phys Ed students to use.

The intersection of Sheila's life and mine took place during a rehearsal of Handel's *Messiah* with the Student Choral Society. We were thrown together, so to speak, because we both had a voice which was so *basso*, it was almost *profundo*. Like a low-slung overfed dachshund, our voices would hug the ground. Sheila and I would sing 'Let us break their bonds asunder,' and we would burst into a fit of giggles. How we would have loved to be able to sing soprano parts like Gill Stevens from the Conservatorium of Music, for when she sang 'I know that my Redeemer liveth,' her voice would soar, filling the interstices of the College Chapel. It almost brought tears to our eyes.

Once, during those early rehearsals, I lost my place in the script and sang, 'And we like goats have gone astray,' to the great hilarity of the rest of the choir.

The conductor, ever watchful for diction, yelled at me:

'Sheep, Gulja, sheep. Think of merino, my dear.'

Sheila came immediately to my rescue: 'I believe it's goats, not sheep, which predominate in the Holy Land.'

'I don't care,' the maestro was not amused. 'It's what the librettist writes that matters. If he wrote *pink-eyed Himalayan hippopotami*, you will have to sing *pink-eyed Himalayan hippopotami*, and that's that.' His Oxford accent was very persuasive.

I took a great liking to Sheila, and we kept seeing each other in the cafeteria, where she spent a great deal of time in debate with the Arts and Law students. I envied their freedom from laboratory work, their wit, their lighthearted banter. It was during one of those meetings that Sheila invited me to stay at her place to lend her moral support before the examinations.

OVER THE YEARS, I HAD often wondered what happened to Sheila. I was sure she would have fulfilled her mother's ambition of taking silk. She would be sitting pretty by now. There were times when, walking past the Law Courts, I would try to see if any of those women with briefcases looked like Sheila. They all looked the same to me: black tailored suits, black shoes, black stockings. It's the dress code, I reminded myself. I am glad my dress code was not as strict.

Sometimes I tried looking for her in the telephone book, but gave up. What if she had changed her name? And even if she did not, what could I say? Our lives had diverged so much. But there was always in my heart a desire to see her again, or at least to know that she was alive and well and that her kindness towards me was remembered.

One evening I was in the throes of marking the Biology Common Assessment Task. It was well past midnight, and my husband, Tony, had gone to bed hours before. But I had to complete my quota of corrections, otherwise I would not have finished by the deadline. I put the telly on, soundless, with faces and images to keep me company while I cogitated about the grades I was meant to bestow on my examinees. High, Medium, Low, Not Shown. Among some of the criteria the one called *Account of the Investigation* took most of my time. That night's batch of papers were particularly bad. Why had none of these students used a spell check? Not that it would have completely saved them though.

From the bedroom came Tony's voice, annoyed:

'For God's sake Gulja, you're going to be very tired tomorrow if you don't go to bed now.'

'I've still got stacks of marking to do, Tony.'

'Oh just give them all a pass. Just put a few ticks on their paper!'

'I can't do that. This stuff is all criterion referenced.' The words sounded hollow at that time of night

A face appeared on the soundless television screen. There appeared to have been some scuffle with police dragging squatters from a derelict house. The woman who was talking on their behalf had familiar features, but I could not place her round face. Some social worker, or a youth advocate in blue jeans, I thought.

Then all at once it hit me: that's Sheila McAll herself. I shouted out loud. I quickly turned on the volume. Dear, dear Sheila, not black suited at all. Dishevelled, she appeared to have come straight out of a skirmish with a local council on behalf of some youngsters.

There was no mistake, the *basso profundo* was still there.

'We are supposed to have local governments look after our welfare. It's bad enough when landlords don't show any compassion towards the homeless, at least they don't pretend that they are charitable institutions. But the council! These young people have actually painted part of the house, and they are being thrown onto the street without alternative accommodation.'

I was riveted by Sheila's commanding presence. Why was she being interviewed at that graveyard hour? Why was she not on prime time television?

Dear Sheila, I said aloud, as if she were there in the room in the flesh, so it's adieu to parterres and hello to homelessness?

The interview over, I switched off the television, turned off the lights and went to bed, my quota of corrected assignments still unfulfilled. Tomorrow, no that same day, I had seven periods of teaching, a recess briefing to attend in the other campus, and a faculty meeting after school. I would have to find some time, somehow, to photocopy the test I still had to write for my Year 10 class. One hundred and sixty students would be in my classes tomorrow. I hoped the laboratory assistant had all the equipment ready for the first two classes at least.

Normally I fall asleep counting test tubes. But that night I felt immensely elated to have seen Sheila again, after so many years. With a great deal of fondness and nostalgia, I thought about my stay at the McAll's—their wondrous garden, their generosity in treating me, a complete stranger, as if I were their own daughter. I thought of Jack and his sense of humour, of elegant Mrs McAll.

Sheila may not be sitting pretty, but she certainly should be walking tall!

The Extreme End of Summer

The young boys could not have been much older than seventeen. They were carrying surfboards and on their bodies the fine fair hair glistened in the noonday sun. They were the kind of fresh-complexioned youth used by advertising agencies for pimple creams.

'Bludgers!' Sharon uttered, her face showing the contempt she felt for those boys, obviously not at work. She almost spat out the words.

'What makes you think they're bludgers?' snapped Judy. 'They could be uni students. Their year hasn't started yet. Or they're having a break from job hunting. I mean how can you tell?' she continued, annoyed at Sharon's assumption about the boys. 'It's not exactly as if there's that many jobs being handed out on a plate to young people at this time, is there? Besides, you ought to talk about bludging! What precisely are you doing at present? You're not what one might call boosting the Gross National Product, are you? Or nursing, or helping the aged, or planting trees or writing books, are you? You're just sun-ning yourself, and sitting on your big backside and enjoying the lucky country stuff, aren't you?'

'Geez! You must have swallowed a record. All I said was they're bludgers. You can see it on their faces. You don't have to go to university to know what surfie bludgers are. I know.' And with that declaration, Sharon jerked herself into a more comfortable position on the sand and continued to stare at the horizon.

Somehow that conversation stole some of the elation Judy had felt that morning as they had stepped on the deserted beach, where, save for the odd seagull and the roar of the surf, there was not a sound—no traffic, no planes, no radios, nothing. Bludgers, indeed! The cheek of the woman.

Judy's eight-month-old Justin was now pulling them towards the water. She had to be careful he did not put sand in his mouth, or swallow seaweed or seashells. But it was lovely being there enjoying whatever freedom was left to her. The rock pools were so clear that the tiniest fish or crab could not escape detection. She found a small and not too slippery pool, where Justin could sit with water waist high as the waves ebbed and flowed over them.

In a surge of motherly love, Judy picked him up, hugging him, almost choking him. He looked at her, momentarily startled. But then he was used to her sudden emotions. He smiled, reassured, mirroring her own smiling face.

The two of them played in the water, oblivious to everything else, while Sharon sat still, in a kind of sand pit that her cumbersome body had dug. She seemed impervious to emotions, and but for the earlier outburst against the young surfers, she seemed totally impassive. It was as if her massive size provided a buffer, an armour of protection, against any changes around her. Or maybe she was too damn hot to bother. As she shifted from one hot, tired buttock to another, hardly moving at all, she did it so slowly and deliberately that a group of blowflies weren't even disturbed. She did everything in slow motion.

This went on for some time, with Justin and Judy playing in the water, while Sharon sat still, as if meditating nothingness.

All of a sudden Sharon yelled out, 'Judy, look! A bushfire!'

The word 'fire' had such a devastating effect on Judy's mind that she jumped immediately to her feet and, craning her neck, located the thin streak of smoke rising against the sky.

'The car!' Judy snatched the car keys from the pockets of her jeans and without looking at Justin or Sharon, she ran in the direction of where she had parked the car.

'Oh my God, the car!' was all she could think of. 'It's all I've got!' Her purse, her clothes and many of her books were in the car where she had left them when they had arrived at the caravan park the night before. Her car wasn't even paid for. Wasn't even insured. God must be punishing me for talking to Sharon like that, a superstitious streak in her said.

Underfoot, the sand was dry and boiling. She had not realised this till now, because down near the water the sand was wet and cool. The car seemed miles away now, and as she tried climbing the sand dunes, she slipped and fell several times, her hands and feet burning as they touched the shifting sand. The fool she had been to park the car so far away from the beach. The downhill walk that morning was a breeze compared to this painful, searing, almost impossible climb. Slipping and sinking, her feet scorched, her heart thumping crazily in her chest, this must be what it's like to have a heart attack.

'The car! I must save the car, it's all I've got.' All she needed to do was to get to the top of the sand hills and survey the view from there to locate the car.

If only she had brought a towel to wrap around her feet, or even a handkerchief. She thought of taking off her bikini and using it to step over, but that would impede her progress. A few more yards, a couple of infernal agonising yards, and she'd be on top of the dune. Hopping from one foot to another she finally reached it, and discovered, to her immense relief, that the grass fire was quite far away from her car. Down there were acres and acres of bracken fern and the acrid smell of the burnt fronds rose to her nostrils.

Her downward journey was less of an ordeal, as she slid clumsily, assisted by gravity and cooler ground. Her legs shaking like jelly, she drove the car onto the road and on a large asphalt stretch away from the bracken.

Judy then got out of the car and watched the thin smoke quietly rising, occasionally spreading with the light breeze, but noiselessly. She had always believed fires to be noisy, tumultuous things, maybe because of her past experience—her childhood home had been destroyed by fire—which had caused such mental uproar. She still remembered everything about that fire, even the putrid smell of clothes burning, but the noises had also persisted in her memory: fire engine bells ringing, people shouting. The sound of the smouldering Singer sewing machine, which a fireman had thrown out of a window, as it crashed against a tree had made her shut her eyes in pain—all the sewing her mother and her grandmother before her had done all coming to naught with what, she perceived, was a heartless act by the fireman.

No, this was a quiet, sneaky, slithering fire, like a snake in a cornfield.

'The baby! Oh my God! I hope Sharon is looking after him.' Supposing Sharon is too slow to catch him? What if he drowns? How irresponsible of her to leave a child near the water!

Judy ran headlong back to where she had left the others. This way—the way they would have come in the first place had she parked the car where Sharon had suggested—was so much shorter.

All Judy's apprehension dissolved as she saw Sharon playing with

Justin in the rock pool. Sharon's dress was raised above the knee, showing her solid, lily-white legs, covered in sand. Overcome with relief, and momentarily forgetting her recent ordeal, Judy ran towards them, smiling.

'Oh thanks, Sharon! For a moment I was worried he had ... you know, drowned!'

'What, with me looking after him?' said Sharon. She seemed to be enjoying herself too.

Judy lifted her son and hugged him firmly: 'Your silly mother doesn't deserve you. I ran to save the car and almost forgot you. You're lucky Sharon was here.'

That afternoon, after waking from a long siesta, Judy made Justin a bottle, and Sharon sat on the bed, staring blankly into the distance. A cool change had arrived, and rain was pelting down on the caravan roof.

The bush around them now looked drab and desolate—no magnificent countryside this, with majestic gum tree or golden wattles, not even clumps of twisted scrubby tea trees—just bracken fern, engulfing every bit of land, advancing inexorably, devouring what could have otherwise been arable soil. That morning's fire, Judy learnt, was an attempt to clear some of the bracken.

In many ways coming here had been a big let down for Judy. She had dreamt of long walks with Justin in the pusher, a bit of botanising and bird watching, and a lot of reading. Instead she had found herself stuck to the old chores in a space so much smaller than her tiny flat in Melbourne. As well as that, sharing it with a complete stranger who was not much of a companion.

When Justin woke, his nappy soaked, Judy picked him high above her head: 'You silly, silly, sod. You wet, sodden, silly sod! You lascivious, lachrymose little lad, you!' She felt a little self-conscious drooling over her baby in front of a stranger. Her barrage of words however were meaningless to Sharon, who continued to stare and say nothing.

Justin was such a good baby. He slept when she did, woke up with her, and accepted her moods cheerfully. Now he drank his bottle avidly, kicking his legs to the rhythm of his own sucking noises. Judy then put him down on the floor and brought out a few of his toys to play with.

Sharon reclined in her bunk as if she was now a permanent resident, with never a mention of when she was leaving or where she was to go from there. Judy had given her a lift because she had felt sorry for her trying to hitchhike on the highway.

'Be a nice day tomorra,' Sharon spoke for the first time since they had arrived at the caravan. They had had lunch quietly, Sharon sipped her lemon cordial delicately. Funny, how she had a way of eating slowly and almost genteelly, lady like, you could forget her enormous size. Judy, in the meantime, guzzled litres of cordial. The earlier ordeal had left her totally parched.

As Judy reached for the packet of sultanas and dried fruit from the cupboard, it felt so light she nearly flung it out of her hand. 'That's strange,' she said, 'I'm sure I brought a new unopened packet with me.' She looked inside it and it was almost empty.

'Sharon!' she yelled, glaring, 'Words fail me. You come here, inflicting yourself on me, sleep in my caravan, a perfect stranger, then when I turn my back you devour a whole bloody packet of sultanas. Do you realise I had two kilos of fruit in this packet?'

'I haven't touched it, Judy, cross my heart I didn't!'

'Then who did? I suppose the Hunchback of Notre Dame is hiding in this caravan? You're not only a glutton, but a liar as well. No wonder you ate lunch so delicately, while pigging out on my fruit. Sharon I demand to know!'

'Okay, I did have a handful, but that's all.'

'That's all?! Two bloody kilos of fruit. Enough to give you the runs for the rest of the week!'

Sharon shrugged, assuming her distant, vacant stare again. Judy banged the cupboard doors and tossed the cutlery into the drawers spitefully. Justin, sensing his mother's hostility, stopped crawling, clutched his panda bear and started crying.

Judy hated herself for her bad temper, her overreaction. After all, had Sharon not saved Justin from drowning that day? Oh yes, Judy told herself meanly, if it weren't for *her*, I wouldn't have been pushed to be so contrary as to park the car in the middle of the bush.

After a silent tea of toast and cheese, a kind of peace descended on them. Judy sat down and for the first time since they had arrived, did some reading, while Sharon sat on the floor playing with Justin. He was enjoying her company, snuggling up to her, playing hide and seek and coming to her for approval. Had it been another woman, Judy might have been a little jealous. But it was good to see him relate to another person, other than his mother. He had tended to be a little too clingy lately.

Then Justin fell and hit his head against a table leg. Sharon, surprisingly fast, picked him up and he dissolved into tears in her embrace, almost disappearing between her voluminous breasts. And, for the first time, looking into Sharon's eyes he uttered what to Judy seemed like the word 'mum'.

The rain continued to come down heavily. There was no question of going for a walk on the beach. Justin was now all smiles, he and Sharon playing together again as if they had known each other for ever. Judy, feeling more relaxed, grateful that she was able to do some reading. She was also a little contrite for her previous outburst—why did she always flare up so at the slightest provocation? Why didn't she control her temper when things went wrong?

All of a sudden Sharon gave out a cry of pain.

'You alright?' said Judy.

Sharon, bent double with pain, and holding her sides, gasped.

'Would you like me to fetch the caravan park manager?'

'Oh don't leave me alone please!' implored Sharon, obviously in severe pain.

'Do you think it's an appendix or something? Wait a minute, the sultanas might have upset you!'

'Oh please don't go, don't go!' was all she could get out of Sharon. The pain was coming in spasms.

'How can I help you if I stay here? I wouldn't know what to do. I've heard of people dying of acute appendicitis.' Judy, as usual when alarmed, was yelling.

'Please, Judy, stay with me. I think it's due!'

'Due? What do you mean, due?' she screamed.

Sharon did not reply but waited for the next spasm to pass. 'I think I'm having it now. I didn't know I was so close.'

'Having it? You mean here? A baby? Oh my God!'

Justin started to cry loudly as if in response.

'Sorry Judy. I thought it was due in May. Honest I did!' Sharon managed to say between bouts of pain.

'All this time you never said anything. And you were hitchhiking to this place, miles from any doctor, let alone a hospital, Sharon!'

THE GIRL WITH JADE EYES

GRAEME MCEVOY TOOK THE LIFT up to his office on the twelfth floor of the Government Building, as he had done every weekday for the past fifteen years.

As the lift door opened to discharge some people on the third floor, he saw her. She was facing the lift. What she was wearing Graeme did not even notice, for what struck him like a bolt of lightning were her eyes. They were absolutely and indescribably green. He had seen a few beautiful women before, but never anyone with that colour of eyes.

All day he kept trying to remember the precise shade of that tantalising green: no, not emerald, not Irish green, not turquoise, certainly not hazel. The colour stirred in him a vague, pleasant, nostalgic memory which he could not identify.

That day Graeme worked absentmindedly, drank innumerable cups of coffee. He left his lunch untouched, walked up and down the office floor several times, and suddenly in a flash, the name came to him. Jade! His late mother's jade ring! The stone of that ring was, as far as he could recall, exactly the same colour as that girl's eyes.

That evening, when his father was watching television, Graeme crept into what used to be his parents' bedroom, and slowly pulled out the drawer of the dressing table, which stood exactly as his mother had left it ten years before. He unwound the key of the jewellery box— which was also a musical box—and opened it carefully.

And there was his mother's ring, an oval jade stone mounted on silver. He lifted it gently, held it to the light, then put it back in the box and returned to watch television with his father. Barry McEvoy, watching the news in his dressing gown, did not even notice his son's brief absence.

Barry McEvoy had settled very comfortably into his widower-hood, for now he managed to perform all the tasks his wife used to do, as well as having a few other interests, like lawn bowls. He also looked after the garden in such a way that every weed was plucked the moment it emerged, and the edge of his lawn was as trimmed as the neck of an officer on graduation day.

Graeme did not share his father's preoccupation with the garden and never raised a finger to help him there. So when Barry would declare that the daffs were out already, or that the buds on the roses were showing, all he got from his son was a disinterested grunt. Barry was particularly fond of daffodils, for not only did they herald the spring, but they were also resistant to snail and slug, and as an added bonus, they grew of their own accord each year, multiplying tenfold in a seemingly effortless process.

Barry did not care one whit if his audience did not share his enthusiasm, and he continued his conversation just the same.

'Next thing we'll have all the bulbs and the ranunculi blooming. Before you know it, it'll be cherry blossom time again.'

Graeme turned a page of his angling magazine.

'I hope there won't be too many frosty nights,' continued Barry, undeterred. 'And by the way, guess who I met at the shopping centre today? You remember old May Cribbin? Well she's still around. Still the same, wearing that silly old hat and gloves, probably on her way to the pub.'

Graeme disliked the way his father would describe all the boring details of his day, who he met, what Mr and Mrs So-and-so said, or did, at the bowling club, how he got a bargain on a detergent and wasn't going to let that special on toilet paper pass him by, no way, so he bought a dozen of the jolly things. Mind you, he wasn't going to buy peanut butter that week, if they insisted on selling it at ten cents more than last week.

Graeme felt like screaming at his father's old womanly ways, but he was too respectful to do anything other than nod.

Both Graeme and Barry shared the same beliefs. Australia, they both agreed, was the centre of God's own universe. Food was divided into two categories: the Australian and the Poisonous. The two men shared an idyllic image of a typical Aussie—a suntanned, sporty, beer-swigging giant. They themselves were more typically Australian, they did not much care for active sports unless watched on the telly, the sun gave them blisters and beer made them dopey. Yet they both subscribed to this concept of the average Australian with the same faith they had in such things as democracy, decency and justice.

In spite of the fact that they were surrounded by people of many nationalities, they never bothered to think beyond the Chesty Bond stereotype. In Barry McEvoy's mind, for instance, all Europeans were vigorous gesticulators, ate voraciously and lived on past glories of crumbling civilisations.

But tonight, Graeme was far away, dreaming about the girl with the jade eyes. Never had a woman had such a magical, almost witchcraft effect on him. He was now forty-five, and had so far escaped what he believed to be female clutches. And since he socialised so little, he rarely met suitable women. But if truth be known, his life was cushioned by a father who did everything for him and charged him no rent—to leave this comfortable set up for an unknown future would be crazy. His married friends were showing on their lined faces the wear and tear of pregnancies, mortgages, schools, medical bills, babies crying in the night. Graeme often thought smugly to himself, I'm glad it's them not me.

But today he felt perturbed, a sense of dissatisfaction grabbed him, as if he had wasted his life. He looked back on his orderly and comfortable existence, punctuated only by the trivial domestic incidences with his father. A sensible bloke, his father also did certain things now and then that really made Graeme's blood boil. Like emptying the vacuum cleaner bag in the incinerator. And there were times when he felt that if the human race used its resources the same way as his father, it would have become extinct by now. For having lived through the Depression, McEvoy senior believed that things could only get bigger and better all the time, there was no looking back. Abundance was the keynote, to worry about using a bit more gas or water was not only mean, but un-Australian.

Yes, Barry was not what one might call enlightened even by his son's not so rigid standards. The two men had their differences, but there were never any arguments of bitterness between them. After a brief blow-up, they would be back to normal with father and son like two old maids discussing what to eat for dinner, or whether the curtains were due for dry cleaning, or whether to paint the architraves white or cream.

But Graeme had started to become very secretive with the fellows at work about the situation at home—one simply did not live with one's father at his age. Not a full-blooded Aussie. When his work mates became curious, he steered the conversation on to some other topic.

Some were convinced that good old Graeme had a bird established at home, one of those who did all the washing and ironing, but left him free. A cunning old bastard is our Graemie, not at all what he appears on the surface, eh?

Every now and then Graeme would try to convince himself that there was nothing unnatural about his situation. Hell, nothing unnatural about not being married like the other blokes. What about priests? Anyway, wasn't an old bloke entitled to his children's company instead of being left on his own?

On the Saturday, Graeme went fishing with Bruce, one of his neighbours. They drove for hours before they reached their designated spot near Moama. Bruce had never stopped bragging that last year he had caught some fantastic rainbow trout in this rather desolate part of the Murray River.

Perhaps moved by the beauty of the bush in spring, Graeme blurted out:

'I'm thinking of getting married.'

Bruce, shocked, put his can of beer on the ground and exclaimed: 'You must be bloody crazy! You've got no idea how hard it is to get away for a day's fishing when you're married. Bloody hell, you can go fishing every weekend, and don't ask permission from no one.'

Graeme cast a line, saying nothing.

'What would you want to get married for anyway? It's not as if there's not enough girls ready for a bit of fun. Listen to me Graemie, go up North, to Queensland or somewhere, and you'll soon forget this crazy idea of yours.'

The two men then stood silently, watching their floats for any signs of bobbing. Every now and then, a school of miniscule fish would dart about, enticingly, leaving silver bubbles rising in the murky brown water. At times, small river flies would settle on the surface, creating concentric ripples of light that danced and dissolved in the silt below.

But despite the denuded nature of this river bank, it possessed a wild, awesome beauty of its own. Where last year's flood water had receded, roots of the giant red river gums had been exposed, leaving gnarled, rope-like structures clutching for anchorage and moisture. Right here, if you stood long enough, you might have heard the echo of last year's angry river as it roared around this sharp bend. Here, where even the most skilled water skier would have lost their footing, the river looked deceptively placid.

But for those two men, engrossed in their thoughts and their fishing lines, all this savage beauty went unnoticed. They cast several times, Bruce swearing every time the bait disappeared but no fish were caught, for the fish refused to bite that day. However he felt that he had done a good deed for mankind by giving his mate some sound advice. Graeme would thank him one day. Marry indeed! Mad! He just didn't realise how lucky he was.

Three months later, Graeme married Natasha, the girl with jade eyes. She was a White Russian and they were married in an Orthodox Church and bought a cream brick veneer house in the outer suburbs. Natasha had always wanted a cream brick veneer house, so Graeme bought one for them. Also she insisted on choosing the one with a photinia hedge which turned red when you clipped it, and with a pittosporum tree smack in the middle of the front garden, but no other trees. Oh no, she wasn't going to let trees cast shade into the house. Natasha detested dim houses, for she had spent her entire childhood in houses with dim interiors and grey façades, and had not come all the way to this country to live in a dark house.

Small World

It had been a trying winter. Madeleine had boarded buses steaming with wet raincoats and dripping umbrellas. Cigarette smells hung like damp washing around one's head. The coughing, sneezing and grinding of gears as the buses laboured up steep inclines had been very annoying.

But it was the driver of the 5.45 who usually spoilt the day. A nervy man in his fifties, he always insisted that the stop-bell should be rung only at precise points, not before, not after. And if newcomers to the bus pressed the bell a little too hard, well, hell would break loose. It was, however, for the passengers who did not have the exact bus fare that the driver reserved his homily around the themes of selfishness, lack of consideration and blatant rudeness.

Regular customers, like Madeleine, knew his specifications and regulations and followed them completely. They knew that when he got upset he was likely to do such things as scrape the bus against the traffic lights, or even worse, make hasty turns, sometimes against oncoming vehicles. There was no knowing what an upset driver would do. Their lives were in his hands.

At times, the passengers, feeling antagonised by him, began to talk to each other. Those people would normally mind their own business on public transport and stare out of the windows rather than try to catch each other's eye. Now they shared the same reason for raising an eyebrow, suppressing a smile, or fuming with indignation at being put in peril: the driver of the 5.45.

Today was a particularly lovely September afternoon. Madeleine noticed that narcissus plants were already in full bloom in gardens, and, from the golden wattles, clouds of yellow pollen with almondy perfume wafted into the bus every time the door opened. Spring was definitely here.

Madeleine had another reason to be in good spirits, because, as from today, she was on holiday. She always took her annual leave about this time. The firm she worked with was too busy at Christmas, and all the resorts would be crowded then. Besides, her mother refused to go on long train trips in summer, it was too exhausting, and there were too many near-naked girls on the beaches.

'Lovely afternoon isn't it Mrs Wilson?' Madeleine said as she sat down near a vivacious older woman who had spoken to her before. Mrs Wilson did not look her age, nearly eighty and well-dressed.

'Yes, about time too. We've had a bad winter alright. The boys at the weather bureau have been getting more generous with their temperatures lately.'

Madeleine smiled and nodded her head.

'Have you got a steady boyfriend, dearie?'

Madeleine blushed a little and shrugged her shoulders, 'Not really, but it doesn't worry me.'

'Oh you must! At your age. Do you want to keep working all your life?'

'I don't mind,' Madeleine lied. 'After all,' she continued, 'half the women at my work are married and have kids.'

'Shocking isn't it, for a woman to have to leave the kiddies to go to work. But you'd only have to see the prices of food and petrol, you can't blame them. I'd hate to be raising a family at this time.'

'I know.' Madeleine did not particularly want to continue on this topic of conversation.

They stopped talking for a moment, holding their breath, watching how the driver was to manoeuvre the bus around a sharp corner. Everyone usually sat very still when they came round this blind corner. They were always relieved when they passed it.

Almost to break the tension and to change the subject of steady boyfriends, Madeleine said, 'I'm on holidays now for four weeks!'

'How nice! Are you going away?'

'Yes, mum and I are going to Perth by train.'

'Beautiful place, Perth, hardly ever rains in spring and summer. The sky is always blue and clear, and some of the wild flowers at this time of year are out of this world. Best time to go to Western Australia.'

'Really? Have you been there?'

'I was born there, and spent some of my happiest years there. Of course them days were different, before the war, like. My father used to take us swimming in the Swan River, bless his soul!'

'It'll be the first for me, going to Perth. I'm really looking forward to it. We've got relatives there.'

'Tell you what, you must go and visit Rottnest Island. Very pretty, only the sea can be a little rough at times, but you'd be able to take it!'

'We're staying with an uncle, mum's brother, in Cannington.'

'Cannington? I know it very well. Whereabouts in Cannington, if you don't mind my asking?'

'Fulham Avenue.'

'No! That's where we used to live! Fancy you going to Fulham Avenue, Cannington! Of all places on earth.'

'What a coincidence. I'm so glad I talked to you today.'

'I'm even more glad you did. I'll never forget that street. Our next door neighbours were called Crouch. Lovely people they were, the old man was a pastor or something. Very kind gentle folk. Generous to a fault.'

'No! They're my grandparents! They're dead now and Uncle Peter lives in the same house. Mum was a Crouch before she married.'

Old Mrs Wilson was so overcome by this discovery, that she turned around, grabbed Madeleine by the arm and hugged her.

'So you must be Connie's little girl! Fancy that! And all this time we've been catching this bus and not knowing.'

Madeleine, too, was overcome by this revelation. But Mrs Wilson continued,

'They were so very kind to me. We were Catholics, and in those days there was a lot of bigotry around, and we weren't supposed to get too friendly with Protestants, you know, it was almost sinful. But your family were so terrific, we never thought of them as different, just very good neighbours.'

'How nice!'

This was too exciting a revelation to leave it at that, so Madeleine accepted Mrs Wilson's invitation to have a cuppa with her, alighting at a different stop from normal. She also promised to give her a 'big surprise'.

'Oh I can't get over meeting Connie's little girl, Mrs Wilson kept repeating loudly to herself, as they walked towards her house, not far from the bus stop.

'I won't keep you long! I'm sure your mother will understand. When are you leaving for Perth?'

'Tomorrow afternoon.'

'That's just lovely! You will have a great time there, I'm sure. When I was a little girl in WA I was a bit of a wild thing. A bit of a tomboy, couldn't sit still. I still am in a way, only I have much less energy. My mother used to send me to the Crouch's to get rid of me, I s'pose. They had a good influence on me, I behaved like an angel for them. I'd run errands and help Mrs Crouch, your grandma, as if I was their own child. And they'd feed me and give me things. Your mother was just a toddler then, and I'd watch her sometimes. I was very happy in them days. We didn't have much then, no telly only this old radio and we sometimes sat around watching it. They used to have funny things on the radio then.'

Madeleine was getting a little impatient, and now that the initial excitement had dissipated, she was anxious to see what Mrs Wilson was going to show her

'Yes, lovely folks they were, you know, they even cooked fish on Fridays just for me, being a Mick as I was in them days, it was a mortal sin to eat meat. Well, one day, as I was sweeping the kitchen floor, I remember it as if it was yesterday, pink lino with yellow flowers on it, very pretty. I stopped to pick up the dustpan, and there was this ha'penny. I put it in me pocket and thought I'd give it to Mrs Crouch. But somehow, I don't know what came over me, I didn't. I just kept it. But I never spent it.'

'Why not?' said Madeleine.

'I don't know myself! I suppose I felt guilty and that if I'd spent it, I would never be forgiven. Funny thing though, it wasn't as if they ill-treated me or anything like that, so I can't explain what came over me. I sometimes think that as children we always thought finders keepers sort of thing. Later on when we came to live in Melbourne I kept it as a souvenir, to remind me of my happy days with Mrs Crouch.'

'But now that's past isn't it, surely you don't still feel guilty for something you did such a long time ago?'

'No, no, just wait till I tell you the whole story,' Mrs Wilson said, busying herself making a cup of tea, while Madeleine walked around the lounge room which was comfortable but quite shabby. On the mantelpiece were a smiling Mr and Mrs Wilson on their wedding day. There were several pictures of a girl and a boy, presumably her children.

'And where are your children now?' Madeleine called out.

'Oh, Lora and Jimmy? They're married and live in Melbourne. They hardly ever come and see me. Only Christmas and Mother's Day. They stop for a couple of hours, that's all. They're always too busy. Everybody's got a washing machine and a dishwasher and all sorts of things, but everybody's too busy to visit their own parents. Terrible! When I think how my grandparents lived, surrounded by kiddies, and here I am on my lonesome, I think there must be something wrong somewhere.'

'Yes. I quite agree. Look here, now that we know you live so close, we can come and visit you, and you can come to our house. You and mum can talk about the old days. Mum will be delighted, I'm sure!'

'Yes, I can't get over this coincidence, what a small world!'

'I'm all ears about the story of the halfpenny, Mrs Wilson. What happened then?'

'I kept it, as I said, after all these years. Of course you couldn't buy much with a ha'penny. Last Christmas, when my son Jimmy was down here, he happened to set eyes on this blessed coin. I'd never told anyone about it. Not even my husband. He died years ago, loved the bottle, and I had a hard life with him, you know.'

Mrs Wilson could see that Madeleine was getting a little impatient so she continued with the story.

'Well Jimmy asked me if he could take it. I said, certainly not! But he said, you're not a coin collector so what will you do with a ha'penny? I said I want to keep it for sentimental reasons.'

'I see,' interrupted Madeleine. 'He must have been very honest, otherwise he might have taken it without telling.'

'Oh no, Jimmy has his faults, but he is very honest. Mum, he said to me, this coin is as rare as chooks' teeth. It could be worth hundreds if not thousands of dollars, think of what you could buy with the money, he said. Oh no, that would be stealing, it's not mine to sell, I told him.'

She went up to the mantelpiece where, among the china figurines, the faded cloth flowers and dozens of other knickknacks, she found a small blue vase with a fluted edge. She placed her fingers in it, but her face registered disappointment.

'Oh dear, don't tell me that Jimmy took it after all!' she said to herself.

Madeleine just sat there sipping her tea, wondering if her mother was worried about her, and thinking that perhaps this story was just some kind of a fable or a ploy by Mrs Wilson to entice her to her place. You never know what these desperate lonely people can get up to at times, she told herself. But what about the Carrington story, and how else would she have known that her mother was a Crouch?

Madeleine saw her disappearing down a long dark corridor, talking loudly to herself: 'I must have hidden it somewhere, I'm getting really silly these days. Forgetful. Where did I put the blessed thing?'

Madeleine thought about all the things she could be doing at home, last minute things before she and her mother went away. Perhaps she should go out and find a telephone booth and tell her mother where she was. Mrs Wilson, she knew, did not have a phone.

Just as she rose to excuse herself, Mrs Wilson reappeared, her pale blue eyes smiling, her hand held out.

'My dear, you are looking at an authentic 1923 ha'penny which, according to Jimmy, and he knows a lot about these things, is worth a small fortune. Take it, it's yours …'

'—Oh, no, I couldn't …'

'—Only make sure that you and your mum come and see me when you get back from Perth.'

Through a Fence Darkly

Mrs Winston was a wisp of a woman, but even as she held open the shabby fly door, she had a certain imperiousness about her. Later on, when I saw her body lying on the road, with clothes dishevelled and stockings torn, I remembered this, our first meeting:

'Yes, what can I do for you?' The voice was firm and aloof.

'I'm Maria, and we've just moved in next door.'

Poor and pregnant, standing in the penumbral light of the verandah, I asked on which days was the rubbish collected, please?

'The *garbage*', she corrected me, 'is removed on Mondays and Thursdays. Winston is the name. Mrs Winston.'

Often I would see Mrs Winston watching me as I walked through the front gate, past the neglected flower beds and the overgrown lawn. Frequently, I saw her down the street, with not a hair out of place; she would be wearing a cotton floral dress, very fashionable at the time. She had white accessories: gloves (in that heat, but they were mandatory for elegance in those days), white hat, white handbag.

I realised after a few weeks of occasional meetings in the shopping centre that Mrs Winston never carried a shopping bag, nor pushed a shopping jeep. Some women of her generation were driving their old perambulators, redolent of babies of the thirties and forties, but now full of shopping and the odd dog.

Mrs Winston's gloved hand would point at the loin chops in the Fair Dinkum Butcher's shop, or at the spuds in Cardamone's Fruit and Vegetables, but it would never establish contact with the goods themselves. The delivery boy would then bring them all to her house. The 'delivery boy' was the generic name she gave to a small army of men and boys who knocked on her door to bring anything from chops to eye drops. I knew, because she talked about the 'delivery boy' as if he were her own personal valet—loyal, discreet, and not likely to jeopardise his career of carting stuff for her by arriving late on her doorstep.

One day I invited Mrs Winston for afternoon tea—after all it was the neighbourly thing to do.

'What nationality are you, dear?'

'Maltese,' I had answered. The disapproval meter on her face dropped a few noticeable notches.

'You must be a member of the British Commonwealth, like us,' she smiled.

The day of the afternoon tea with Mrs Winston turned out to be a hell of a day. A hundred degrees in the shade, and with morning sickness, even so late in my pregnancy, worse than ever.

There were scones and jam tarts, honey, cream, orange tea-cake, don't spare any trouble, and three types of Twining's. Don't let the Commonwealth down, dear. Those pink lands on the wall maps of my childhood classrooms in Malta were all watching to see if I was worthy of the privilege.

Carefully ironing the tablecloth and the serviettes, and dusting the few pieces of secondhand furniture, I kept an eye on the clock and the oven, while the temperature in the house rose.

My next problem was how to foil the ants. As long as I kept them at bay till the end of The Afternoon Tea, I would have been quite happy. It was, however, a ceaseless struggle. Armies of them would rise from the ground continuously and, slowly but inexorably, cover everything. And it was not just in the kitchen, for if there was a crumb to be had in the bedroom, they were not going to miss the opportunity of carting it away.

I waited for Mrs Winston, absolutely exhausted by the heat and the anti-ant vigilance, surveying the table of scones and other goodies, and shooing any flies which inevitably entered the house through the torn fly screens.

Two o'clock. Two thirty. Three o'clock. Still no Mrs Winston. The doorbell never rang. Fearing that she might have forgotten our date, I decided to go and fetch her myself. Gravid and grumpy, I knocked on her door.

'Come in dear, door's open,' a strangely hoarse voice beckoned.

Mrs Winston was slumped on a chair, surrounded by a sea of mostly empty beer bottles. The room, the whole house was indescribably smelly and untidy.

'Mrs Winston, I was expecting you to come and have afternoon tea with me!'

She looked at me with sleepy, red eyes.

'You must be the Eye-talian lassie next door. No, no,' she reprimanded herself, 'from Malta, that's right. How else could she speak English so well?'

She said all this with a triumphant smile on her face, as if dredging all this knowledge about my nationality was a test she managed to pass in spite of her completely inebriated condition.

'But I made a lovely afternoon tea for you, Mrs Winston. Scones, and jam tarts and cakes. I baked them myself for you this morning. In this heat,' I said almost in tears.

'I had visit-it-ors, I had visit-it-ors all day, as you can see. I could not get rid of them. What was the name, Mary, no Maria. That's why I thought you were Eye-talian.' Speech slurred, she continued her soliloquy about my nationality.

'How did the afternoon tea go?' my husband asked me when he came home from work.

I told him what had happened.

'You went to too much trouble, Maria.' The British Empire had never bothered him, obviously. He was born in Melbourne of Italian parents, so he would not have understood my feelings about the matter. 'Don't worry, we'll eat it all ourselves.'

When I brought baby Lino home from the hospital, Mrs Winston leant over the wire fence and asked me:

'What did you have, dear?'

'A boy,' I said proudly. 'Just what I ordered,' I joked, still walking on air, in spite of the sleepless nights.

She ignored the joke and said, 'A boy! What a shame, what a crying shame,' unaware of her pun.

'Why?' I was more than a little taken aback by her attitude.

'They break your heart. I know. I had three sons, you know. Gone. Not one of them comes to see me. Not one!'

'I'm so terribly sorry to hear that. Where do they live, your sons, Mrs Winston?'

'Oh, all over the place. But I haven't seen them for years. Not even a card for Christmas. Best if we don't mention them again.'

By now the Afternoon Tea affair had been forgotten. Motherhood was, for me, a twenty-four-hour job, where sleepless nights merged into dopey days, full of feeding baby, changing nappies, and keeping the ants away. I had terrible visions of them rising and eating my baby when I was asleep. I had once seen a film about ants covering an injured antelope and not resting till every bit of it was carried to their nests.

By now my fear and hatred for ants was only matched by their cunning ability to foil every method I used to keep them at bay. Use pepper, someone had advised. So I sprinkled it everywhere. This did not seem to bother the ants at all, as they meandered through the trail, effortlessly avoiding the pepper powder. Put a saucer of water under each leg of the food cupboard. Oh yes, this veritable moat would stop them, I noted gleefully. But no, they found other bridges from the wall to the shelves, anything, even a small piece of paper left carelessly touching the walls was a highway to the food.

I broached the subject of the ants with Mrs Winston as she was waiting for the bus one morning, attired as usual in her elegant clothes. The weather had turned chilly, and she was wearing a smart woollen suit, yet strangely enough she had the same accessories of white gloves, shoes and handbag she had worn all summer.

Mrs Winston ignored my baby in the pusher and gave me this piece of advice:

'Poison, my dear, poison is the only thing that works with the little beggars. Excuse the language. But just get some poison from the hardware shop. My gardener does it for me, and I haven't seen an ant for years.'

My gardener. Naturally, one does not garden with white gloves on. So it had to be the gardener. Wait a moment, though, what was he doing these days if the garden was so overgrown with weeds you could barely see the standard roses?

But she must have read my thoughts.

'I should have said my *late* gardener. Poor man, he had a coronary and dropped dead. I cannot find another one quite like him.'

'Look, we'll do your lawn ourselves when we do ours. It's no trouble at all, Mrs Winston!'

'Oh, no, no, no, no, no. I wouldn't hear of it. This other fellow is supposed to come, one of these days. Oh here comes the bus.' And, almost as an afterthought:

'Don't let that babe of yours wear you out too much. You do look like death warmed up!'

Although my relationship with Mrs Winston had improved immeasurably by now, there was always the feeling that it had to stay at arms length. At the back of my mind there was my vision of her, slouching, drunk, on her couch, and I knew that that person was not to be resurrected. So our conversations had to be very general and impersonal. The fact that her three ungrateful sons never came to see her was a source of some pity on my part.

'They could be in jail,' said my husband. Not a sentimental man, he dismissed my concern as unnecessary. I should mind my own business.

'What, the three of them?' I retorted.

'It happens, you know, maybe they killed their father, that's why she gets pickled every so often!'

'Oh, you are just so cold and logical, aren't you?' I said. Becoming a mother had made me over-sensitive perhaps.

A few days later (or was it weeks, because it is now over twenty years since Mrs Winston entered and left my life after such a brief friendship), she turned up at my front door with a neat little parcel. She had knitted the most darling pink matinee jacket for my baby. It was one of the sweetest, prettiest things I had seen, with pearlescent pink buttons and satin ribbons to match.

'Look, Maria, I'm sorry about the colour, but he can wear it inside the house.'

'Oh, I don't mind the colour at all, it's really gorgeous, thank you so very much!' And I really meant it.

I made as if to hug her, but she winced slightly, so I did not persist. I was delighted that she was thawing a bit towards me, and even though she never called Lino by his name, I didn't think she hated him. She was just bitterly disappointed that he wasn't a girl.

One afternoon I saw a man mowing Mrs Winston's lawn.

'G'day,' I called. 'The garden is looking good now. I can see the roses!' Mrs Winston's predecessors must have been lovers of roses, and there were some beautiful long-stemmed ones I would not have minded myself.

'Her ladyship's having a party', he informed me. 'The house is so full of distinguished guests, it's not funny!'

'Really?' I fell for it. He laughed, pointing at his forehead.

'It's all in her sick head. She's on her own getting stuck into the amber fluid again.'

My face must have indicated to him that I was not amused, because he went back to his mower straightaway. I was not about to make fun of this poor woman behind her back with this smart aleck.

If, in recounting that period of my life, the first magical days of my motherhood, I am painting a picture which is black and white or even sepia, then I'm misrepresenting my story. My life then was full of colours. There were quince trees, nectarines, apples and plum blossoms which delighted us in spring, and the corrugated iron fence separating the two humble houses was festooned with climbing red roses, wisteria, honeysuckle and morning glory.

'You call that fence nice? It's leaning at an angle of sixty degrees! It's positively dangerous.' My husband threatened to pull it down as soon as we could afford to replace it.

'What about Mrs Winston? She may not be able to afford her share!'

'She'll have to give up her grog won't she?'

I did not speak to him for a whole day after that.

We had other neighbours too, besides Mrs Winston. Mrs Brown, who, in spite of her gout, was ever so cheerful. The Sicilian family opposite us who grew forty kinds of oregano for a front lawn. The Greek family with the plump children and the iridescent blue Falcon, the 'trim, taut, terrific' model. The Polish couple a few doors down cooking their national dish, *bigos*, which you could smell from everywhere. And though we all lived very private lives, unlike my childhood in Malta where we all lived a neighbourly life, here in this inner suburban street, we did share a few experiences: when our pets got run over, or when the kids broke a window playing cricket. And we were still grieving over Harold Holt's tragic disappearance; even if we ourselves had not gone all the way with LBJ, the man's demise had left us all very sad.

Mrs Brown was a wonderfully garrulous woman, so I once mentioned Mrs Winston's ungracious sons to her. 'Oh, she told you that tale too, did she, Maria?'

'Why, isn't it true?'

'It is, and it isn't. She did have a few children. Two or three. But they all died at birth.'

I remember that statement vividly even today. It was like being struck by lightning. I can still see Mrs Brown's corpulent figure framed by the yellow lacework of her verandah, as she delivered this devastating fact about our neighbour. Two or three dead newborn babies. My legs felt like jelly.

'And what about Mr Winston?'

'Oh God knows. He shot through, I believe. I think he went back to England or something. He couldn't cope with it out here.'

DID MRS WINSTON THROW HERSELF out of the moving tram deliberately, or was she too confused to wait for the tram to stop in High Street? Though I have had nightmares about it, seeing her body flung against the pavement (I will not say 'gutter', it would offend her), I am glad now that I had seen her. For even in that dishevelled state, and with her shoes muddied, her face covered with blood, she had a certain regal air about her, diminutive though she was in her white gloves and matching handbag.

The Longest Night

I wake up with a start. The liquid crystal numbers on my clock radio tell me that it is too early to get up yet: 4.44 am.

I am absolutely awash with sweat, and suddenly it all hits me: *must write that email, must write that email, must write that email …*

I don't remember how I found myself in bed. Someone must have carried me home from the pub. I vaguely recall first trying to get warm, then trying to cool myself. I have thrown away the thick winter blankets onto the floor.

My husband, tired of the tossing and the moaning and the mumbling and the pulling of bedclothes, must have abandoned the matrimonial bed for a single bed in a quiet spare room. I don't blame him. My breath must stink from all the grog I drank last night.

What I do remember with a shock is that horrible email I had written …

My head is a balloon ready to burst. Now, that's wishful thinking! Balloons don't have a tormenting brain inside them. Nor are they usually attached to plumbing with anti-peristaltic action, like my head is at the moment. I am feeling so nauseous that unless I write that letter of apology, I'll be vomiting my head off.

Must write that email, must write that email, must write that bloody email.

I'm even saying it loudly. Like the Hail Marys in the rosary … *now and at the hour of our death, Amen.*

Dear Don, I mentally write, *I don't know what came over me … you are the nicest possible boss I have ever had, could ever dream of having … please ignore, delete, obliterate that obnoxious email that someone forced me to send you, virtually at gunpoint. No, not exactly at gunpoint, but just about … You know what a sick sense of humour some of the people at work have … remember what they did at the last Christmas party … well, please then … I am so ashamed of myself, so sorry and remorseful … I will do anything to make up for …*

The room where my computer is housed is so cold, it could double up as a fridge. So I wrap a warm dressing gown around me and turn on the machine.

Instead of the welcoming WINDOWS XP, I get an unfriendly dark screen, with a reprimanding message. As your computer was not turned off correctly, some or all of your files may have been lost …

Shut up, I yell at it. *Don't give me any of that crap! I have to write an email, now!*

'Are you talking to me?' My husband, woken up with the noises I have made, is in the corridor. I have managed to disturb his sleep even from where I am.

'No darling! It's this shit of a computer here!' I reassure him. 'It won't start!'

'What are you doing on the computer at this hour of night?'

'I'll tell you in the morning!' I am unnecessarily brusque to my husband. He senses that I am not in a conversational mood and scuttles back to bed.

I restart the computer. This time it's even worse. The screen is blank. Unresponsive. Dead.

In my dazed state and my panic, I pull all the plugs out of their sockets. How this irrational act is going to help me, I don't know.

After a few tries, I'm connected to the Internet and my email box. The unread emails start filling the screen. Many of them unsolicited, some obscene, some boring, some expected. The one I'm looking for is not there.

He must have been so offended, so put out by what I wrote that he has not answered. If I am sacked, it would be well deserved. I have gone over the top. Crossed the line. Sunk all my boats.

Dear pisspot, I had written in my inebriated state, from the internet café near the pub, while all my so called friends looked on and cheered my audacity, my courage, I foolishly thought. And how stupid of me; why did they not write it themselves, if it was so clever? Because after a few glasses of wine I had become so full of bravado, so fearless, so dimwitted …

Still, the unread emails keep rolling in. The Viagra peddlers have got a new address which is not yet on my black list. *No, I am not interested in increasing my penis by four extra inches, thank you very much*, I tell my computer loudly.

There is a stack of undeliverable mail. In my lack of concentration I often leave out letters or full stops, use dashes instead of underscores, and make other small mistakes which any postman would ignore. But which the tyrannical Almighty Infallible Unforgiving God of Email Addresses rejects every single time.

Hello! There's an undeliverable address which looks familiar. I cannot believe my eyes. And my luck!

The very same email I sent to my boss last night in my inebriated state. I had misspelt his name!

So my boss never got that email! I do not have to apologise and grovel after all. I do not have to start looking for another job.

'What was all that about last night?' asks my very patient husband on his way to the office.

'Oh, some deadline I had to meet,' I lie, as I kiss him tenderly.

Later, overcoming my tiredness, I get ready for work. I wear my smartest suit. My highest heels. I take my most expensive handbag to work. I notice that today is the shortest day of the year: June the twenty-first. It could have turned out to be my darkest!

I smile sweetly at my boss. *You look nice today, Janet!* He has noticed my unusually elegant outfit.

3

SHAFTS OF LIGHT

THE PLATE

PATRICE ALWAYS MADE SURE THERE were no fingerprints on the glasses before she poured drinks, or any tiny scraps of food from previous meals on the plates. She did not trust the dishwasher to be as meticulous in this respect, and examined each piece of cutlery and crockery carefully before putting it away in the cupboard, and then again even more closely, when she was setting the table.

So it was a great shock to her, when, just as the table for afternoon tea was complete with its vase of flowers, gingham tablecloth, matching serviettes and tea cosy, there was an explosion and the plate containing the hot scones shattered into a thousand pieces. All of a sudden there was a shower of green glass bits, which, in the twinkling of an eye, disappeared as quickly as they had been formed. She imagined shards so sharp and long that had she, or God forbid, her neighbour Betty, been sitting at the table, they could quite easily have pierced their hearts.

What shook Patrice was the speed with which this extraordinary event had happened. She picked up some glass pieces from under the table, and some off the chairs, yet she could only retrieve what she estimated to be less than ten percent of the plate. Look though she did everywhere, or almost everywhere, for she still had to be ready for her friend Betty to arrive, she could not find any more bits of green glass. It was as if they had turned into gas and floated in the atmosphere.

Now she had more things to worry about, as well as the sponge cake to be iced—she prided herself on the perfection and smoothness of her icing. There was nothing more embarrassing than lumpy icing on a cake. Patrice had regarded with disdain the efforts of some women who had the audacity to present for cake stalls ghastly things covered with coloured sugary lumps. Couldn't they see the unsightly finish of that icing or were they blind? She had once presented a cake, a very rich and expensive fruit cake, which had a tiny flaw in its icing cover, and she spent the rest of the time apologising for its imperfect finish. Yet these other women would go around expecting everyone else to praise sloppy handiwork just because they used free-range eggs, or whatever was trendy.

While most women of her age would have lost their youthful figure, Patrice seemed to have kept hers. It was not difficult to identify her as the girl in the picture on the mantelpiece—her tall, slender frame topped by a blond bouffant hairdo, her long legs in knee-high boots teamed with a brief leather mini skirt. Now, of course, the skirt had been replaced by well-tailored slacks, and the boots by sensible shoes.

'You're a great clothes horse!' her husband used to tell her every time she put on a new outfit, a compliment she remembered with bittersweetness, even after Ben had gone—into the arms of some nubile woman he met at work.

'Much good did that do me!' she would reply loudly to herself. When her husband left, she felt faded, like the colours on her china after having been in the dishwasher so many times. Life, she began to realise, was like a giant dishwasher, silent, but pervasive, relentless, and unyielding. Skin, bone, hair, organs, all losing their essential hue and tone. But not her figure, for she had kept her slenderness.

Nowadays she looked forward to the afternoon tea and a chat with Betty. They had not had one for a while, Betty having had a series of minor ailments. Patrice felt sorry for her, long time widowed by a husband's cancer. They had a kind of affinity with their single status being forced upon them, and rendering them members of the same club as it were. Besides, Betty was the only neighbour in her street who had lived in the same house for as long as she.

Patrice regarded herself as well above her acquaintances when it came to sweets. She had seen *real* food on her trips to France— where she had done a course in *patisserie*. Her eyes had seen culinary marvels none of her neighbours could even begin to imagine. She had watched a French chef who, more like a magician, had turned a saucepan of sugar into a large rubber band, which he then proceeded to cut in strips and to plait and create all kinds of amazing confectioneries. She watched him explain, in his heavily accented English, the elastic properties of albumen in the egg. Yes, he told them with a glint in his eye, the old *hegg* has more wonderful possibilities than to be merely fried, boiled or scrambled.

When Patrice visited the Musée d'Art de Chocolat at L'Isle de Tarn, her eyes were opened to the magic of artistic food. In those clean, cold rooms of the museum, not only were there life-sized statues of people and beasts totally manufactured from chocolate, but the grand piano itself was one solid chunk of the delectable stuff, with its keys looking exactly like any Steinway. So, when her friends gooed and gaahed about some chocolate cake—out of a packet if you don't mind—she just smiled smugly to herself.

Today, to complete the settings, there was the tea caddy to

be taken out and displayed carefully on the table, and not just anywhere. This tea caddy, covered with pictures of prim Japanese girls in kimonos under apple blossom trees, Patrice had inherited from her mother. It was often the talking point of her afternoon tea sessions, especially when the conversation topics were heading towards some embarrassing theme. At times, running out of subjects to discuss, she would draw the attention of her guests and elaborate on the history of the colourful caddy and the conversation would revive again.

She had thrown out the scones, even though there was no evidence of broken glass on them. However, the sponge cake was still on the bench and not on the table when the accident happened. It would be okay—she could use it. Besides, it was far too late to bake another.

'What absolutely gorgeous flowers, Patrice, you really have a wonderful flair with roses. I hardly ever get a bloom from mine!' were Betty's first comments, much to the hostess's delight.

If only she knew how much time Patrice had spent that morning— those roses had to be picked early before the dew dried on the petals, and only the perfectly formed ones were to be used. Then she had to examine every leaf and petal: it would be the height of rudeness to have a vase of flowers with aphids and thrip dropping on the table or, worse still, in the cups. How mortified would she have been!

The afternoon tea went well, with Patrice never breathing a word to Betty about the incident of the shattered plate. What would Betty think of her as a housekeeper if she knew? Besides, Betty might be worried that there could be bits of glass embedded in the sponge cake which they were going to share! What if there were indeed bits of glass which would penetrate her friend's intestines? How could she ever forgive herself?

For weeks later, Patrice kept inquiring—albeit discreetly—how

Betty was, dreading any news of tummy aches or nausea or any other condition that could point to some piece of glass ingested by her friend. But no, luckily, nothing other than the odd migraine to which Betty had been prone for a long time. Patrice also looked up several medical books in the Library to see if swallowed glass could harm, or even kill in such miniscule quantities. It appeared that she did not need to worry because the sharp ends of glass would, according to one reliable source of information, become quite blunt in the stomach juices.

Long after this incident, while Patrice would be sweeping or vacuuming, or removing stains from the carpet, she still kept finding tiny bits of glass, embedded in the carpet loops, or stuck to the leg of a chair or a table, under the refrigerator, even between pages of books on the bookshelves. Once, while looking in the encyclopaedia under the letter R for Rhodesia, to her great surprise, she found an elongated piece of glass right where the map of Zimbabwe was, as if it was a bookmark! It was uncanny finding this object, like an arrow, a needle, pointing exactly to where she wanted to do her search.

And it was not only in the dining room—where the accident had happened—that she continued to find these remains, but all over the house. She even found several pieces among the fluff balls under her bed.

In a way it was a relief every time she picked up a piece of glass. She would then save it in a jar kept high up in her pantry. However, the amount of glass she found was much, much less than the plate which had shattered. It was a source of dismay for Patrice that the jigsaw puzzle was unlikely ever to be complete. Where, oh where, had all that glass gone? So much for the theory that matter could not be created nor destroyed! Some time in her past, a Science teacher had told them that glass is really not a solid, but a supercooled liquid. Maybe therein, she thought, might lie the explanation of the disappearance of the exploded plate. Maybe the liquid glass evaporated with the explosion. One of these days, Patrice would tell herself, she would find the rest of the plate behind something, a cabinet, a sofa …

'HI, MIRANDA, I'VE JUST HAD a crazy afternoon tea with Patrice,' Betty told her sister over the phone, the day of the exploded plate. Betty and Miranda were very close and had several long conversations each week on the phone. They knew the minutiae of each other's day, but this time Betty was bursting to tell Miranda what happened.

'You know that old dear, Patrice. I think she's really losing her marbles! I had a cuppa with her today! And guess what, she used salt instead of sugar in her cake. It was dreadful, awful! But I didn't want to hurt her feelings, so I just ate the icing and stuffed the rest in my handbag. I always take that large old bag, the one that used to belong to mum, when I go to Betty's. You know she didn't even notice that I wasn't eating the cake! Poor thing, I think her eyesight, too, is going. She raved on about that silly tea caddy of hers—her mother brought it from Japan or somewhere. She doesn't realise that you can buy one exactly like it at the two dollar shop!'

'Didn't *she* realise that it was salt in the cake?' Betty could almost see her sister on the other side of the phone, frowning, puckering her face as she was wont to do when puzzled.

'No, well, as a matter of fact she's always on some diet. She didn't eat anything. I told you, she's as thin as a whippet, but thinks she's fat!'

'So why do you keep going to see her if she's so mad? Go to the gym or do something else.'

'I feel sorry for her, you know, she's lonely, and quite a kind soul too, and she's never been herself since her husband ditched her. She used to be quite outgoing, travelling, getting all dressed up. They were quite a good-looking pair in their heyday.'

'Well, weren't we all …'

'Oh, and I must tell you what else happened at Patrice's today! Just as I was about to sit down on the couch, I saw this broken plate, well, the best part of what used to be a green glass plate. I couldn't believe my eyes. At first I was going to ask Patrice what on earth was a piece of glass plate doing among the cushions on the couch? Then I said to myself, no, she'll be so embarrassed that she'll carry on and on, and never stop apologising. It would have ruined her afternoon.'

'That must have been a bit of a worry, so what did you do?' said Miranda.

'I just stuffed it in my bag and when I got home, I threw it in the rubbish bin, with the cake.'

'I suppose you did the right thing, better than let someone injure themselves with it.'

'That's what I thought, too. I'm sure Patrice won't even miss it.'

The Butcher

'Sulk, sulk, sulk, all you've done is sulk,' Sally said, while banging the last pieces of cutlery from the dishwasher into their drawers. She was feeling so irritable that she put them into their respective compartments without checking that they were properly dry. Usually she hated wet cutlery in drawers.

Her husband, Peter, sat with his back to her, pretending to read the paper. She knew that he was pretending to read, because he never bothered with the *Weekend Magazine*. It would have been different had it been the Sports section, which he devoured from cover to cover.

Still he did not answer her accusation.

'Why are you like that, ever since this afternoon you've been sulking all the way. I could see that something was eating you. Even the way you parked the car. Why, what have I done?' she asked, this time yelling at him.

'It's the way you were all over that Jack fellow. That butcher friend of yours,' he blurted out at last.

'Oh God, Peter, I can't believe it! You're not jealous, are you? He's almost old enough to be my father!'

'What's age got to do with it? You obviously find him very attractive. It really made me sick.'

'Peter, get hold of yourself! He was my butcher, our butcher for years and years, surely that must mean something. Some, some gratitude, some respect.'

'Oh goodness me, Sally, I've been going to the same bank for decades now. I am not about to fall over and kiss the bank manager when I see him in the street.'

'But that's different. He does it for money. Jack did what he did, well, because he liked it. He was, more human, you know what I mean, a very kind and considerate person? He always knew exactly what each customer needed.'

'You mean to say that our chops and sausages were personalised? Come on Sally, admit it, you always had a crush on him. He's only a butcher, after all, but the way you talk about him sounds as if he's some kind of a brain surgeon!'

'I tell you what, you're not far wrong. If some surgeons are like butchers, Jack was more like a surgeon. The way he cut meat. Trimmed the fat and gristle. No frayed edges on steak, no bone chips on chops. Such clean cuts, such precision!'

'There you go again. *Dr*, or is it *Mr*, Jack, now joining the ranks of the medical profession. No, sorry, the ranks of the surgeons! Heart surgeon is he or what?'

'Stop being so sarcastic, Peter. As a matter of fact he knew a thing or two about anatomy, and not just where loin chops came from.'

WHEN PETER AND SALLY HAD BOUGHT the old weatherboard house, it was all they could afford, and only with a second mortgage from an extortionist finance company. They were surrounded by European migrants. Big-boned Latvian women who carted large sacks of sugar from the grocer's shop, and shaved their little boys' blond hair 'so they won't get no lice from the other dago children'. There were dark Sicilian men who planted oregano, tomatoes and potatoes on the front lawn. Polish families who cooked *bigos* and the entire neighbourhood smelled of cabbage for days. 'But what can you do, these New Australians have some strange habits!' was the common theme from little old ladies perambulating dogs in their old prams. Those were the sixties, and the trendies had not yet invaded their working-class suburb.

Sally herself would almost faint when passing by the deli—the smell of *parmigiano* and *mortadella* was so overpowering. She had never tasted those products and only much later, in her forties, did she venture inside the shop to get some olive oil.

Once she had asked the butcher for thirty ox hearts for her Biology classes. There were no laboratory assistants in her school in those days. She had to take care of all that herself before each practical lesson. Jack had made sure that not only were the ox hearts there on time, but that they were as intact as possible.

'I'll make certain those hearts will have no aortas missing, or deep gashes down the centre.' He knew that if those specimens were mutilated, the students would not be able to observe the actions of the heart properly. Most butchers did not bother with such trivial matters.

Look at the valves, Sally, aren't they marvellous? What an amazing structure. It's like a powerful pump, as you well know. These tickers here must have gone through some action!

What was so great about Jack the butcher was that not only did he understand what he was doing, but he absolutely loved it. When Sally had mentioned this to her husband, he dismissed it as being another ploy on the butcher's part, a way to ingratiate himself with his customers, so they keep coming to his shop.

'A butcher's a butcher, and that's that.'

According to Peter there was nothing to it. Butchers just cut and weighed meat and made a living. So what, if some were more friendly than others.

'It's not that, darling, you can see the way he cut the meat, the way he handled the meat even. He certainly knew what he was doing, and what's more, he loved it.'

Sally had seen butchers up to their elbows in livers and kidneys, which used to make her sick. Ever since she had studied physiology she had stopped eating any offal, but with Jack it was different. You knew that he had removed the nerves and the offensive parts, and left only the good, wholesome and edible sections.

'You have to be careful with this stuff,' he once told Sally. 'It's so rich in protein and other nutrients that bacteria love it and multiply easily in it. I'd never sell livers which are more than a day old. Some butchers cheat and put all sorts of preservatives and chemicals to make it last longer, but I don't believe in that. You can kill a child or a frail and elderly person by feeding them liver which has not been properly handled.'

When Sally was a student she had taken a holiday job as a laboratory assistant in a hospital. One day she ventured into a room full of glass cases—rows and rows of ovarian cysts in formalin and glycerine, it nearly made her vomit. But she didn't, or she would have lost her job.

There was a particularly large cyst which had been excised out of a Greek woman. Had the woman waited another month, the surgeon told her, she would have died. Why had she waited so long, he asked the woman.

'Proffessorr,' she replied in her strong accent, 'my doktorr kept

telling me that it's all in my head, and that I should take some tablets and go back to work. I told him it's in my belly, not my head.'

She had to have a total hysterectomy. The husband, who spoke very little English, was furious when he learnt that his wife could not have any more children. She, on the other hand cried with relief, as she already had six daughters, but the husband was expecting a son, or two. He had already paid a lot of money in gifts, and sent these to his village in Greece, to the patron saint of fertility. So, understandably, he felt cheated by all: his wife, the surgeon and the saint in his village.

Now the poor woman's huge ovarian cyst, complete with both her ovaries and uterus were on display, pickled in Pathology, proud specimens for the surgeon who had performed the operation. That cyst was quite something: they called it the Marilyn Monroe, there were others, the Brigitte Bardot, the Twiggy—they all had a nickname. When she saw them she felt sad and sorry for the women, even though the removal of those growths meant in many cases the saving of their lives. She was sure that the husband of the Greek woman would not have been amused at the sight of his wife's organs displayed in those glass cases, and would have felt humiliated by the display of his wife's lost fecundity.

Once or twice Sally felt tempted to talk about her laboratory experience to Jack the butcher. She thought that, of all her acquaintances, he would be the one to understand. Thankfully, she never did. Besides, his shop was always full of women, some of them Greek. It would have been in very bad taste on her part. She would have appeared as if she was making fun of them.

Ten years ago, just before Christmas, Sally had gone to stay with her sister, Carla, in the country. Carla was expecting what already had been confirmed as a stillborn child. Yet she could not be delivered of it. It was a most hideous time for her, knowing that the child inside her had ceased to move, and yet she had to go through childbirth and pain as well. Everywhere she went there were people who, in trying to be kind, made such comments as: 'Are you still here, Carla?' or 'That child of yours is a bit lazy, isn't it?' not knowing that all the time she was expecting the child to be born dead.

So Sally took time off work and left her own children. All her Christmas preparations were abandoned, so she could be with Carla. The child, a boy, cruelly enough, was born on Christmas day. The sight of the dead child in her sister's arms had completely ruined Sally's Christmas and she had not even rung up home to give her greetings.

What she hadn't realised was that the Christmas ham she had ordered from her butcher, and for which she had not paid the last instalment, was delivered to her door with a note which, to her husband, sounded like some kind of a love letter:

To the lovely Sally, with my compliments. I hope the ham is succulent enough.

Her husband had been so enraged when he read the note which Jack's assistant had delivered with the ham, that he threw it away in the garbage bin.

When Sally returned home from her sister's place in the country, she was utterly drained by the experience. Christmas was well and truly over and the decorations had been pulled down. Peter was a practical man and had noticed that the pine needles from the live Christmas tree were embedding themselves in the carpet, and the coloured lights were getting dusty, so he cleaned everything up on New Year's day.

Both of them had forgotten about the ham: she that she had ordered one, and he that, in a fit of jealousy, he had thrown it away.

Some days later, Sally went back to buy some steak from her

butcher and told Jack where she had been; he never mentioned the ham or the money that she still owed to him. She had completely forgotten about it all, but when she did remember, and asked Peter how the ham was, he mumbled something like: *what ham?* and nothing else.

Peter did not need to worry for much longer. To Sally's great disappointment Jack sold his shop and retired to another suburb. She never saw him again, and every time she passed by his shop she used to feel a tinge of sadness. The shop became a furniture store, then a greengrocer's, then a dress shop, then a jewellery shop and now it was a café. None of the other businesses seemed to have done well, and they each closed down within a year of their opening. That morning, when Sally and Peter met Jack in the city by chance, she was delighted, but at the same time taken aback at Peter's hostile reaction to their fond greeting. A few days later she had forgotten about Jack, but her mind kept returning to the Greek woman and her husband.

•

A Terrible Thing

There is something especially enervating about the pale blue of the sky on a hot day in the inner suburbs. It is as if all the heat generated by the factory ovens and hamburger shops rises and hovers obstinately above, adding layers of oppressive translucency to that sky.

Stella was feeling quite exhausted from a sleepless night and the humid heat. Her life on the eighth floor of the Housing Commission flat would have been quite bearable, even given the heat, but not for her four-year-old son. Johnny was a severely hyperactive child, who had seen various psychologists and other experts. They all said that he was intelligent, but highly strung, which didn't require a university degree to work out. Stella experienced Johnny's moods a thousand times a day.

Johnny was now sleeping, tired from the heat and the effects of a sedative.

It was a dreadful thing she had done, Stella told herself. Now that the place was quiet, she began to feel the full meaning of what she had intended to do.

Johnny had banged his head hard on the wall because she had refused to give him lemonade, a drink designed to make him even more hyperactive. No, he did not want the other drink. His father had insisted on buying the lemonade, against Stella's wishes, for why should he suffer because of the child. Wasn't life hard enough for him as it was?

Stella had given in, against the dietician's advice, and after drinking a whole glass of it, Johnny flung the glass against the fridge where it smashed to pieces and left a dent on the door.

'I must calm myself before Philip comes home.' In half an hour, her husband would arrive from his night shift, and it was her turn to leave for work.

'WHERE'S JOHNNY?' WERE PHILIP's first words.

'He's asleep. How about asking how I am for a change. I've had a rotten night.'

'Same here. I wonder how long you would last in my work with the noise and smells. I'd rather be home sleeping at night.'

'But at least you don't have to put up with Johnny as much as I do. He's always so much worse when you're away.'

Philip sat at the small kitchen table, still wearing his greasy boiler suit.

'Why can't we move from this place? Why can't we live somewhere at ground level?' she begged.

'We've gone into that many times, Stella. We can't afford it.'

'But now that we both work we can.'

'Yes, but we won't be able to save for a house if we rent somewhere else.'

Philip looked tired, and ate the snack she had prepared for him with no enjoyment at all.

The tram to the hospital where she worked went past their place. She was so agitated that day that she dropped her handbag and its contents spilled on the grubby floor of the tram. The other passengers looked at her, saw how disconcerted she was and looked the other way. Anyway, it was too hot to bother. Besides these New Australians are used to the heat, she'll be right.

It was a terrible thing to do, she kept telling herself, what had happened that morning.

In the steamy kitchen of the hospital, the clatter of cutlery, the large stainless steel saucepans, and the milling about of the other workers made her forget her problems for the time being.

'Stinking hot day out there, isn't it?' Marge said. 'You look like death warmed up, Stella. I thought you liked the heat!'

'I'm OK Marge.'

'OK my arse. Is it little Johnny again?'

Stella nodded as she wheeled out the patients' lunch trolley, trying to avoid showing her red eyes. If the boss saw her crying again, she might think that she was unfit for work. Plenty of others could take her place, waiting in the unemployment pool.

Marge ran after Stella and grabbing her by the arm, told her, 'Look here, we'll have a little talk later after you've delivered the lunches.'

Stella nodded and continued down the shiny corridor. She looked at the clock. She was already late. She hurried along, and turning around a blind corner, she ran straight into her boss, Mrs Gilbert. The impact sent some plates flying, the lids clattering along the spotless floor. Sweet corn and peas scattering on the wax polished surface, gravy splattering on the white walls.

Mrs Gilbert in a fury picked herself up from a most undignified position.

Later on, among the slop buckets, the pyramids of dirty dishes, Marge O'Keefe's rotund figure assumed almost regal proportions, and her words of advice had a ring of authority about them. People in aseptic clinics often proffered advice to Stella, but she didn't think they really understood. Marge had had a hard life, and to Stella, her words were more believable than when they came from a lab-coated expert. At least Marge did not make her feel inferior, and even though she kept reminding Stella of her youth, she did not treat her like a child. There was something wholesome and honest about Marge.

'Trouble with you, Stella, you got married too young. When I was your age, my biggest problem was deciding which boyfriend to go out with next Sat'dy night. Instead, you're killing yourself slaving in this kitchen and battling an unmanageable child,' she had told her. 'But it's no use talking to you like this, the deed's been done. But I'm surprised an Eye-talian like yourself hasn't used your mamma a lot more.'

'I told you many times, Marge, I'm not Italian, I'm Maltese.'

'Okay, same thing. As I was saying, your mother could help out a bit. Or Philip's mother could.'

'Philip's mother lives too far away and Mum has enough problems with her health. Johnny would kill her.'

'On the contrary Johnny would make her forget herself. You said that she was a bit of a hypochondriac. All she needs is someone to care for.'

'But Johnny is not an ordinary child. He wrecks everything.'

'Yes, but she could relieve you for an evening, every now and then. What sort of a life is that with both of you tearing off to work round the clock?'

STELLA HAD ALWAYS KEPT THE balcony door locked. It was said that children had fallen from Housing Commission balconies and killed themselves. The only time she kept the door open was when Johnny was asleep or not at home. Some nights she would sit in the balcony and contemplate the city on the horizon, with its strings of street lights and its huge neon lights. They had been objects of wonderment for her parents who had arrived in this country from a small village in Malta.

When Philip and Stella had been given this flat, they were told that they were lucky to have such a fantastic view of the city skyline. But now she was not sure it was worth the risks.

'You must not let that Gilbert woman upset you, Stella. You must stand up for your rights. She talks like that to you because you're timid. She would not talk like that to me, or to someone who was born out here. That's the kind of bully she is.'

'Yes, but it was my fault. I ran into her.'

'Everybody makes mistakes. She herself burnt the food for the whole floor. This was before you came. She's still here.'

In Stella's mind Johnny was yelling, 'I hate you mummy, I hate you! I want you to die so I can get lemonade and sweets. I'll take the money from your purse and go to the shop and buy lollies and chocolates and ice cream. Daddy loves me. He gives me lollies when you're not looking. I like daddy. I wish I could go to work with daddy …'

'I did a terrible thing this morning, Marge.'

Stella had stood shaking, watching Johnny throwing cushions and toys all over the flat, running around pulling everything from its place. Flinging things. She had left the balcony door shut, but not locked. Since it was forbidden territory, the balcony had attained for Johnny a special fascination.

She watched him trying the door handle, his face showing pleasant surprise to find that it was not locked, looking furtively around. She pretended that she hadn't seen him. She felt as if her feet were nailed to the floor. A horrible wicked thought crossed her mind. A thought she had at times entertained. What if he falls from the balcony and kills himself? Then perhaps she could have some peace. Her life could perhaps assume some order. She and Philip could start all over again. It would be so easy …

'Why don't you take a few days off and rest?' Marge suggested.

'How can I have a rest with Johnny's constant demands? And where can I go with a child who wrecks everything?'

Stella could almost hear the judge acquitting her. A harassed mother. Victim of circumstance. An oppressively hot day. Several sleepless nights. She forgets to lock the balcony door. The boy is too quick, and before she could reach him, he's over the top. Instant death. Not guilty.

'You don't know what I nearly did this morning, Marge. He could have killed himself. And I didn't try to prevent it. I just stood there. On purpose. I didn't lock the balcony door. I mean I was actually plotting Johnny's death. Can you imagine?'

She pretended she had not seen him, and kept preparing Philip's food. She saw him taking a chair to the balcony and standing on it. She saw him leaning as far as he could over the top of the railings. For a moment she though she'd faint. A certain malign force seemed to have nailed her where she stood. It seemed an eternity. But it must have been a matter of minutes.

Stella fell sobbing in Marge's arms. The day had just been too much.

'Yes, but he's alright now isn't he. Don't let it upset you any more, dearie.'

'He could have fallen down. I could have prevented it. I didn't try to stop him. It would have been murder. I had … wanted him to …

fall.'

She wiped her face. Her handkerchief was sopping wet now.

All she wanted to remember was the sheer relief when she saw Johnny come down from the chair, and in a matter-of-fact way declare, 'You know, Mummy, it's the first time I saw the roof of the tram. Wow, it's b-i-g!'

A Small but Annoying Mystery

Francis was making a costume for the school play. A munchkin costume, to be more precise, for one of the little actors in the *Wizard of Oz*. Her daughters had left the school a long time ago but she had continued to be part of the mothers' club's activities, and for several years she even served in the tuckshop a couple of times a month.

Now Francis did not like sewing, in fact she hated it. But when she was asked to lend a hand with costumes, as there were so many of them to be made —hundreds in fact—she had foolishly agreed.

Francis had not touched a dress pattern since she had made them at school in Malta, when her sewing teacher had shown the class how to draw patterns first on graph paper and then on thick brown paper. The students had to make block bodices which were the bases for blouses and shirts, as well as bloomers and pleated skirts. She had not only botched up each and every one of the patterns but also the calico objects themselves. She failed dismally the subject of Needlework.

Now, confronted with flimsy, ready-made patterns, she felt terrified. What if she misinterpreted the markings on the patterns?

What if she cut both sides the same, or sewed them back to front, or worse still, cut the fabric wrongly and ran out of it? How could she explain her idiocy, her ignorance, to Maureen in charge of costumes, a woman with such an ego and such an aggressive personality that she terrified the mothers every time she opened her mouth?

Yes, Maureen, of course Maureen, absolutely right Maureen, were the only expressions the woman elicited when she made a proposition, or a demand or a request of the club members.

Fortunately, Francis' husband Fred was going to be away for a few days, so she could leave all the sewing on the dining room table and not disturb the arrangement. She never bothered to cook when Fred was not home. She would just knock back a sandwich and a bit of fruit, and save herself the trouble of washing any dishes.

Francis cleared the large polished table, and opened the pattern packet with its filmy contents, carefully, almost with reverence, as if Maureen herself were watching her. She then laid each piece, one by one on the table: left sleeve, right sleeve, right and left fronts, back, skirt back, skirt front ... carefully. Oh yes, this was no straightforward costume, there were epaulette-like things, several layers of sleeves, bits hanging from the waist, others from the neck and the skirt. How on earth was she ever to complete this task without completely ruining the material or have a nervous breakdown or both? Even when she thought the pieces she needed were all laid out before her, there were other bits of tissue whose place in the garment she could not identify immediately.

She started reading the instructions. *Selvage* side (oh yes, how she knew the selvage side and the weft of material, that she had learnt very well from her Needlecraft teacher, God bless her). *Nap*—at least she did not have to worry about the nap in this piece of cloth. *Darts*— dotted lines, oh yes, you fold, but do not cut along the dotted lines.

Cut on the *bias*. Yes, she knew that term well. How many yards of bias binding had she ruined in her past? How many of them had started their life as pure white and ended ignominiously as grey warped bits, full of brown needle holes, having been sewn and unpicked so many times? *Pleats*—you allow three or four times the width for the pleats. *Hem*—oh she did not know exactly what length hem she had to cut. Silly of her not to have asked the measurements of the child who was to wear this costume. All she was told was to use the medium measurements. But there were four sizes, and she did not know whether it was the second larger or the second smaller that she had to use.

She might have to ring Maureen after all, who in her imperious, disdainful way would most probably tell her: *Weren't you listening when I briefed you about the costumes?* Or *didn't you read the instructions on the notice board?* Or worse still: *You're supposed to have studied at the university, can't you read instructions?* Maureen prided herself with being self-educated and had nothing but contempt for university degrees and those who had them. And how can she, Maureen, depend on helpers if they failed to read notices or to listen to her instructions? Hasn't she enough to do, organising hundreds of costumes without having to answer every possible trifling question?

Maybe, thought Francsi, if I cut the garment a little bigger, then perhaps trim it later? But no, she had to get the size right or else nothing would fit. All the little frilly and dangly bits would simply not fit in the marked triangles and dots on the pattern.

She was feeling the beginning of a headache. One of those headaches which felt like a knife thrust through her brain. A migraine in fact, where she would have to lie down in a dark room and forget about everything, or else get so sick that she would start vomiting.

There was nothing else she could do but go and lie down and leave everything on the table. As she lay fully clothed on her bed, with the blinds down and the curtains drawn, she tried to relax and dispel the worry she had about the task she had to do. But instead she kept blaming herself for being impulsive enough to put herself out for this job. A voice in her head kept reminding her that she was utterly hopeless when it came to sewing, so why did she say yes?

Francis did finally fall asleep and when she got up, a little groggy but with her headache mostly gone, she realised that while she'd slept the weather had changed and the wind had risen.

'Oh my God!' she remembered that the windows of the dining room had been open. 'The pattern!'

The pattern pieces she had so carefully placed on the table were mostly gone. Blown away. Some were stuck among the foliage of trees, some had fallen on damp ground, and some were on the floor. In a state of utter panic she tried to reconstruct the set of pieces. But all she had found were one right sleeve, part of the skirt, part of the back. All the frills, trimmings, collars, and other accessories had gone, being so much lighter, they had blown away completely.

'What am I going to tell Maureen? She'll kill me!' she said loudly to herself, wringing her hands.

When Francis summoned enough courage to telephone and tell Maureen what happened, she was surprised at how sympathetic was her reaction. 'Don't worry, Fran, just bring the materials and the fabric back to the school tomorrow. Janet is making several of those costumes. She'll whiz them up in a couple of hours. One more costume won't make much difference to her.' Oh yes, said Francis to herself, Janet the wizard.

From then on, Francis could feel the ice in Maureen's voice every time they bumped into each other. 'She thinks I manufactured that story about the patterns disappearing,' She ventured to tell her husband one day.

'Let her think that. Thoughts can't hurt!' Fred could not imagine what the fuss was about.

'You don't understand, do you?' muttered Francis, knowing that confiding in Fred about such matters would not bring about any solace. It was, in the scheme of things, a trifling matter, no one had been hurt, no one had uttered any criticism, not to her directly anyway.

A COUPLE OF YEARS LATER, Francis was dusting the top of her dresser. She had to use a ladder, because the top of this cupboard was so high that even by standing on a chair she could not reach it. The last time her husband had done this job he had been shocked at how much dust had accumulated there over the years.

But this time Francis found something much more interesting. The left sleeve, the back, and the dangly bits of the munchkin costume pattern were there, every single missing piece. All covered in dust, but unmistakably the missing pieces.

Michael

Tears of frustration and anger welled up in Edward's eyes. The effort of trying to remember the name of the nice man who had just spoken to him and had said goodbye so nicely, exhausted him.

Margaret rearranged the rug which had slid down his knees and was touching the grass. She tucked his now almost useless legs, thin and twisted, inside the soft tartan rug, released the brakes on the wheelchair, and wheeled him into a sunny spot. The afternoon breeze had turned into a cool wind and she looked worriedly at the gathering clouds promising rain.

'Do you want to go inside, Dad?' she asked.

These afternoons usually began with much promise of fresh air, fine scenery, a picnic, and many encouraging words:

'You look great Dad! We're going in the gardens now! You'd love the rhododendrons at this time of year! I've got some lovely goodies for you Dad!'

But they invariably ended with father becoming tired and grumpy or by being cut short because of some thunderstorm.

This time Edward indicated very emphatically that he did not want to go indoors.

Some days his dementia did not bother him at all. He found the daily routine in the nursing home boring and not worth recalling anyway. His nurses, whose names he forgot the moment the last letter was uttered, flitted about like shadows around him.

Edward had fought the onset of this condition, had done so with a fierce determination worthy of his younger days as an academic. He had, before he was put in this mansion peopled with ghosts, carried a pen and paper with him, to make sure he'd remember who was who, who did what, and where he'd been. But in the end, he found himself losing all the bits of paper, and, worse still, writing so illegibly that all he was doing was compounding his confusion.

'Did you like the cakes I made especially for you, Dad?' Ever the dutiful daughter, whose Sunday afternoons were dedicated to her father, Margaret was getting a little hurt by Edward's increasingly unresponsive, almost ungrateful manner.

He looked at her, eyes glazed. He had not really grasped what she meant.

'What cakes, dear?' he said, speech slurred and slow.

'The ones we've just had for afternoon tea,' she said, re-opening the tin still containing some of the lamingtons and small pink cakes she had baked the night before.

'Oh yes, yes, yes!' not wanting to be caught forgetting again. The tin was an unusual semicircular container, which had belonged to his late wife, Elaine. It was on the verge of rusting, but its familiar geometry had a soothing influence on him, why, he could not remember. Elaine, like her husband, had frugal tastes and preferred to spend any luxury money on such things as books and music. Her possessions had lasted for decades and this was one of her 'things' that had her character, as it were, inscribed on it.

Margaret shook the crumbs off the groundsheet and proceeded to read her book, leaving her father to his own thoughts. It was so exhausting having to explain everything and repeat things so many times that she often got hoarse on these afternoons. Lately, she had decided to let him have a little nap in his wheelchair and make sure he was comfortable.

Edward did not mind a bit of quiet contemplation, and had he been able to express himself, would have said how much he looked forward to Margaret coming to take him out in the gardens every Sunday. She took him to a different garden every time, knowing how much he loved the outdoors.

A patch of sweet williams caught his eye. What colours and varieties they have nowadays! In his time he was lucky to get anything other than red and white. He had loved gardening, which blended well with his job as a botanist. He had written books about ferns and conifers. His own garden was quite magnificent, and Elaine had pleaded with him to have it entered in the Open Garden Scheme for visits by the public. But he had adamantly refused.

'I don't want any bloody strangers trampling around in my garden,' was his excuse.

When Elaine died, Margaret was teaching overseas, and as he was riddled with arthritis and could no longer bend down, Edward had engaged various gardeners. But he always managed to antagonise them by calling them stupid and ignorant, and suggesting that they did not know the first thing about plants. There were scenes of shouting and altercations when a young gardener had planted dahlias on a south-facing slope, mowed the weeds rather than pulled them out, and added insult to injury when he threw certain very hardy weeds into the compost heap where they thrived.

Nowadays Edward's mind flitted from one thing to another

without any chronological order or logic. At times he remembered how he had met Elaine, another Australian, under a giant banana tree in the sweltering humidity of the hothouse in Kew Gardens. They had burst into laughter at the irony of it all: two Aussies studying in England, meeting in tropical conditions, while outside the misted glass walls a freezing rain was pelting away. Perhaps it was the warm, nostalgic feeling engendered in them on that cold February day, and their collective homesickness that made the first meeting particularly exciting and memorable.

Both Edward and Elaine were doing postgraduate work in Botany—he as a taxonomist in Oxford, she as a physiologist at Cambridge. They had been perpetually poor and cold, and their romance across the two English university cities sustained them in their loneliness. They got married quietly in London, before they took up positions in the same department of the same university. Thankfully for their marital bliss, their separate focus of research kept them apart for the best part of each day.

Edward had a temper—it was probably the main reason for his lack of promotion in spite of his publications and his work. Elaine had been promoted several times and was associate professor just before she died, whereas Edward was still a senior lecturer. Fools never got off lightly with him even if they happened to be his superiors. He had a sharp brain, but also a sharp tongue to match.

'Who was that tall American, Margaret?' he asked suddenly, as if pulling a thread from a tangled spool of memory.

'I don't know, you had a number of tall Americans working with you, Dad.' Startled, and slightly annoyed to be interrupted from her reading, Margaret was often confronted with such questions about the past. Her father now only talked about the past.

'No, no, he was in genetics. He had done something really famous about something.'

'How do I know which one you are talking about. It's *ages* now!'

'You knew him. He smoked a pipe and wrote his name on his milk bottles in the fridge.'

'Dad, I forgot his name, why did you want to know?'

Edward looked ahead of him, his eyes focussed on some point on the horizon, and ignoring his daughter's annoyance he continued:

'What a bloody fool he was! I asked him to look after my indoor plants at one stage. He killed every one of them. He might have been a brilliant geneticist, but what a dill he was when it came to growing plants. He killed every one of them. And do you know Margaret, he even killed an aspidistra? *Now what sort of poison did you put in the water to kill an aspidistra plant?* I asked him. He didn't like that!'

Edward chuckled so loudly, that a dog passing by stopped momentarily to look at both father and daughter.

Margaret did not reply, but put down her book, carefully noting which page she was on. She was in for one of those convoluted, frustrating conversations which led nowhere. She had heard the story before, and it brought back the memory of her mother's distress at the way her father used to embarrass her in front of his superiors. They were the sort of episodes which had cost him several promotions. Elaine was certain that that was the reason they had stopped being invited to informal faculty parties. She had felt that those gatherings were so important to keep in touch socially with the other academics.

Margaret herself, who was much more like him than her mother, had admired his fearlessness, his assertiveness. Besides, he got to spend more time at home with them than with his colleagues. When she was little, she had adored him.

'Dad, you were very rude, and naughty,' Margaret said, with some amusement, at the remembrance of her spirited father and his exploits at the Botany school. She had to keep reminding herself that the wreck in the wheelchair was once a respected academic with an encyclopedic knowledge of scientific facts, and an entertaining lecturer, whose sense of humour helped to swell the number of students who enrolled in the subject. But not in the last few years—his lack of promotion and his critical attitude had made him unpopular.

'You are an insolent man,' Edward continued, mimicking an American accent. 'And I have no time for such trivial things as watering plants. I am a geneticist, not a horticulturalist!'

He was feeling immensely pleased with himself, as if by dredging all this from his past, he was winning another victory against his nemesis. He felt like a man who, lost in a desert of forgetfulness, suddenly comes upon an oasis of crystal clear water of memory. He chuckled noisily, unashamedly, tears filling his eyes again with the joy of recollection. He cried easily these days, something that he had never done much of in the past. It was as if the reservoir of tears had been so full that with his approaching end, he needed to empty it frequently.

Now dark clouds were starting to gather, and suddenly he felt very cold. His quest for the American's name forgotten, his mind switched back to the few minutes before, when he had bid goodbye to that other man, that nice young man who had shaken his hand and left him and Margaret on their own. The sudden greyness of things had brought into focus the original question which had bothered him earlier on.

Yes, what was his name? A feeling of despair, a sense of panic came over him. Trying to remember what it was that he needed to recall was now one of his most frequent and angering thoughts. *Who was he, who was he, who was he?*

'Who was he?' he uttered aloud.

Margaret, thinking that he was still referring to the tall, American, and getting a little worried about the impending storm rather impatiently answered that he must have known dozens of tall Americans. She slowly collected her belongings, folded the groundsheet, adjusted the tartan rug around her father's legs and disengaged the brakes.

'No, no, no, no,' her father protested, 'who was that nice young man who was talking to us here, before?'

Margaret stopped in her tracks, shocked at the preposterous nature of the question. She turned to face her father, holding the wheelchair with both hands to prevent it from running away down the steep incline.

'Yes the nice man with the, with the, glasses … who was he?' he repeated.

'Dad!' Margaret almost screamed at Edward, her voice trembling with emotion, 'That was Michael, your son. Our Michael. My brother Michael. Have you forgotten him already?'

And with that she turned around behind the wheelchair, and proceeded to wheel her father towards the gate. She began to cry silently, as she had been doing so much recently, her tears mingling with the large drops of rain, which were beginning to fall on them.

A magpie trying to protect its nest swooped over their heads.

The Dream

Dr Robertson was not in the habit of having extravagant dreams. But one night, he did have one such dream, and it appeared so utterly real while it lasted that waking up the next morning was a bit of a shock.

He dreamt that he was walking through an immense arcade with a huge ceiling, highly ornate, and actually a blown-up version of the Galleria Vittorio Emmanuele in the heart of Milan. To his great surprise, when he looked down he noticed that, instead of a mosaic floor, he was walking on turf. Completely weed free, and absolutely flawless turf. All around him were trees and bushes and parterres immaculately trimmed, and perfectly symmetrical. Suddenly he recalled the magnificent gardens of the Peterhof Palace in St Petersburg. And as he proceeded down the steps leading to the central lake, where he somehow expected to find the golden statue of Neptune, he was quite shocked to see the Statue of Liberty itself.

But what provided the most stunning contrast to this verdant scene, were the beds of bright red tulips, exactly like the ones he had seen near Buckingham Palace in the spring. Row and rows and rows of prime red tulips.

How clever, he thought, for all of these to be combined under the one roof! Literally! And what a fabulous dome-shaped roof it was, too. Oh yes, his *cognoscenti* friends would scoff at all this, as an architectural monstrosity. But he certainly did not think so.

He walked on, lightly touching the perfect foliage of the hedges and the faultlessly spherical bushes. He noticed, too, that the tulips were fleshy and superbly formed, untouched by pest or blight. Drops of dew hung on each flower—globular diamonds, tantalisingly close to extinction and tempting to touch.

Dr Robertson did not remember being so elated. But where was he? Was he in Milan, New York, London or St Petersburg? There were signposts at every intersection of the huge complex, but when he went close to read the names, a mist seemed to settle around his eyes, and no amount of straining or squinting could enable him to decipher the writing. He felt a twinge of annoyance, but he soon dispelled it and kept walking. After all, it really did not matter where he was because he was loving every bit of it. The marvel of having all those things together.

So far he had been completely on his own, but as he turned a corner, he saw a shabby old man in a dirty brown suit sitting on a bench. The frayed shirt collar, which must have been white at some stage, was grey and filthy. The man had a week's growth of beard, and his fingers were yellow with nicotine. There were empty beer and wine bottles and cigarette butts on the ground.

Somehow, almost instinctively, he recognised him as an Australian hobo.

I don't believe it, he said to himself. He probably sleeps here at night too! Amazing how the gardeners don't throw him out.

Dr Robertson went up to the man, but the fellow appeared to

be fast asleep, his unshaven face resting heavily on his chest. Not wanting to disturb him, Dr Robertson just stood in front of the man for a short time. This derelict-looking creature was probably in his fifties, but looked older. Dr Robertson also noticed that he had a deep dimple on his chin, and that, in spite of his neglected condition, the man must have been quite handsome.

WHEN HE GOT UP THE next morning, Dr Robertson felt a twinge of disappointment. He had never had a dream so real, with colours so violently and excitingly vivid. He could not identify anything he had heard or seen recently which could have precipitated such a dream. Also, it was at least four years since he had been abroad, and most of what he had seen was well and truly buried in the subconscious by now.

Subconscious! That's right! 'I wonder what old Sigmund would have to say about this preposterous dream and the hobo?' he heard himself saying loudly, almost with a chuckle.

The thought of that unkempt man in such unlikely and magnificent surrounds haunted him. He had not, recently, encountered or treated anyone who had such strong features, such a dimple on the chin as conspicuous as the one this man had.

The day beckoned. It was Thursday, and it was the day when Mrs Steele came to see him. When he had bought the practice in Collins Street from old Dr James, he had, so to speak, inherited Mrs Steele.

Mrs Steele had to have psychoanalysis every Thursday. Or so she believed. He estimated that had she saved the money she had paid to Dr James and now to him, she could have gone on a cruise round the world several times on the QE2 or its equivalent. But Mrs Steele was not interested in travelling, and if she did go away, it had to be for less than a week so she'd be back for her visit to Collins Street on Thursday.

There was nothing essentially wrong with the garrulous Mrs Steele, and if the expression 'it's all in the mind' was ever coined for someone, it must have been for her. Dr Robertson felt almost guilty sending her the bill, but she did not seem to object. She paid promptly and gave him and each of his staff presents and chocolates for Christmas and Easter every year without fail. So he knew that she was a satisfied client.

Mrs Steele was a widow and her husband had made pots of money selling wool. His father before him had amassed a fortune, and as he was an only son, he had inherited everything. Now she had become the beneficiary of all that wealth, and she could virtually do what she liked with the money.

Dr Robertson suspected that it was not so much the visit to his rooms which did the therapeutic trick of keeping Mrs Steele out of what she claimed was depression, but the shopping spree and the lavish lunch in the city afterwards. Still, he was not complaining; the woman obviously thought that sanity was to be worked at, and paid for dearly, and she wasn't going to scrimp. Oh yes, she had to see him each week, even when he threw broad hints of how well she could cope on her own.

'I'm entertaining this evening, and must get some fancy grub from the city,' she told him today.

Dr Robertson had visions of a sedate party with a whole lot of middle-aged women playing poker and reminiscing about the good old days when wool was king.

'To be honest with you, doctor, there's this gentleman called Norm, and he has, sort of proposed to me.'

'Ah, really,' Dr Robertson tried to hide a little apprehension in his voice. So this could spell the end of these long, lucrative Thursday sessions, and the shopping sprees at Georges and Myer!

But he heard himself asking, in a businesslike voice:

'And do you like this man?'

'Well, yes, I do. But when you've lived long enough on your own, as I have, you value your independence a great deal.'

'Indeed!'

'Well, Norm was an old friend of my husband. They used to auction wool together. His wife passed away last year and he was getting, shall we say, a little restless and lonely.'

'That's natural. But what sort of a man is he? Do you think you could share your life with him?'

'Oh, I thought I'd talk about it with you. I was hoping you'd help me make my mind up, you see.' Mrs Steele had always left her big decisions till after Thursdays. She never made a decision unless she talked it over with Dr Robertson.

Dr Robertson shook his head.

'Really, Mrs Steele, I think that ultimately it's your decision. You're the one who has to live with the man.'

But she was not listening. Instead, she was rummaging in her handbag for something.

'Oh, here it is. That's Norm, doctor. Not a bad-looking sort of a chap, is he?' she said handing him a photo.

And staring him in the eye, but with an air of great confidence, and leaning possessively over a gleaming gold Rolls Royce was the hobo himself, complete with dimpled chin.

'Oh!' Dr Robertson could not conceal his surprise.

'What's the matter? Do you know him?'

'Oh, no, no, not really!'

'You had me worried. I thought you went pale for a moment.'

'Oh no, I don't know him at all. He looks well off!'

'Yes, he is. Loaded, in fact. But that's of no consequence to me, as you know, I'm not exactly penniless myself.'

'Certainly not, Mrs Steele.' He couldn't agree more.

Strange, strange, he said to himself. Norm the hobo is alive, and a prosperous wool millionaire, owns a Rolls Royce and is in the process of wooing the matronly Mrs Steele. The next thing he'll believe, if he isn't careful, would be that the preposterous Galleria-Peterhof-Buckingham Palace-Statue of Liberty complex really exists. How absolutely ludicrous.

'Mrs Steele, does Norm have any children?'

'No, he was, like us, childless, unfortunately.'

'Well then you'll find no opposition to your remarrying.'

'Not from that direction. However, I still have to think about it seriously.'

'I'm sure you'll make the right decision.'

'Thanks, doctor, you're very kind!'

Neither sounded very convinced and Mrs Steele left without another word.

WHEN MRS STEELE CAME FOR her usual visit next Thursday, she did not let him ask the question which was uppermost in his mind.

'I had to refuse Norm. It's no use.'

'But why? I thought the … alliance would be perfect. No children, no impediments, plenty of common interests.'

'I know. But that's not everything.'

Dr Robertson was speechless.

'You see, doctor, when you looked at the photo of Norm, a sort of shock came over your face. No, no, don't apologise. You must know something about the man. Don't tell me. I don't have to know what it is. I'm aware of what you, in the trade, call professional ethics.' She chuckled to herself, as if to say that, after all these years of talking to doctors, something must have rubbed off.

'Besides,' she continued, as if she was relieved to have made the right decision, 'I love my freedom, and Norm might not like my Thursday trips into town.'

She Looked in Vain for Fruit that Summer

That summer, that memorable summer which had followed the floods, Mary had looked anxiously for fruit on her trees and on her plants. It was, she realised (but was not game to say it out loud) a sign of her desperate wish to become a grandmother; a wish for pregnancy in her, as yet childless, daughters.

The garden had been a great disappointment. She had covered her precious and expensive gladioli bulbs with fungicide before storing them in the usual place in the shed. When she went to plant them, she found that although they were perfectly well preserved on the outside, they were empty inside. Some clever little woolly bug had seized the opportunity, and, safe from any marauding fungi, had thrived well inside, devouring every bit of the bulbs' flesh. Ah well, this year her friends would have to go without the gorgeous long-stemmed white gladioli she gave them last Christmas. And besides, the water restrictions were getting more severe and it would have been difficult to repeat past years' successes.

Ah, the promise of dazzling, lazy afternoons perfumed by the basil lurking among the bright red *grosses lisses* and the truss tomatoes with their savage Sicilian red flesh! Oh, for the *pomodori*, the golden fruits, the luscious tasty fruits! They had summer inscribed all over their lusty flesh. Those tasteless ball bearings masquerading as tomatoes she bought from the shops were, as her late husband used to say: *senza sapore, e senza amore*, without flavour, and without love.

Each day, starting from September, she had looked for any signs of flowers on her tomato plants. Nothing. Oh it's too early, she consoled herself, the plants are too young. October, a few chilly nights, what do you expect? Tomatoes don't like frost on their leaves. November, and the floods had rendered the garden so soggy that it was impossible to walk around it without gumboots. Tomatoes don't like wet feet. What can you expect?

A few days before Christmas, some smart Alec on the radio wanted to know what to do with her bumper crop of tomatoes! Share them around, you bitch, Mary yelled to an empty kitchen.

Every time her four daughters and their male partners visited her, she made large roast dinners with all the trimmings, which they wolfed down with great pleasure. They mostly cooked vegetarian meals for themselves, and she knew they loved the occasional leg of lamb.

'Mum, you eat too much meat. It's not good for you at your age,' Lidia would invariably say.

'Lidia does have a point, mama,' Giuliana would echo.

Rosa and Allegra usually said nothing, but from their eyes, Mary could see that they, too, were in agreement.

'Bloody hell,' she would tell them, 'I only eat like this when you're around.'

Mary looked in vain for any signs or hints of impending motherhood in her daughters. Nothing. Healthy, fit, strong, what was the matter with them? What was wrong with their men? Have they run out of sperms or something? Their talk was of computers, compact discs, films, overseas trips, restaurants, and parties. She searched in vain for any twinkling in the eyes, or enlarged bosoms, or over-solicitous partners.

None of those. There was the endless talk of holidays, the tennis and the cricket and the cycling each summer. Mary often had to hold her tongue and *not* ask, 'When are you going to start having babies, you lot?' She noticed with alarm the appearance of some grey hair on the girls, and the little patches of pink baldness on their partners' heads. So what, she tried to reassure herself, she had started going grey in her twenties, while her mother still had shiny, fiercely jet black hair. And bald men still could have babies.

When she was not bathing or feeding or medicating her infirm and stubborn mother, Mary spent most of her time in the garden. Or washing the heaps of dirty sheets and towels and clothes. Bizarre isn't it, at a time when she could have been changing her grandchildren's nappies she ended up changing her mother's instead.

The garden used to be a source of great solace, especially in summer. But somehow this time it had disappointed her in lots of ways. Why, what happened to the strawberries this year? They were tiny and tart and misshapen. Some virus, the man on the radio told her, had proliferated in the unusual weather conditions this year. She had planted new seedlings, new varieties with labels promising big and juicy fruit, yet the only red colour in the garden was that of the pictures on the labels.

And this year, not even the birds got a feed of the cherries. One day, the tree had decided to abort every single flower on it, as if to say: 'I will not give you anything this time, so there!'

But the raspberries! How she had looked forward to picking them, to release gently each tender little berry from its soft green cone. The first time she had eaten raspberries, not out of a punnet, but straight off the bush, was in France: they were growing wild on the Route St Jacques. Aaah, the flavour, the texture, the aroma. They're growing in the shade of big trees, she told herself, they should grow well in a south-facing corner in my garden in Melbourne.

She had made sure they were covered by a net this year, and that there were no holes in the net. But no, nothing happened, no raspberries this year, sorry. She tore off the netting to examine closely what was the cause of this infertility. Was she getting obsessed about fecundity? She'd better watch herself! The flowers were there, but in each little bud a fat, succulent caterpillar was quietly eating away the ovary. Protected from the birds by the net, the caterpillars were feasting on her baby raspberries. Damn. Damn. Damn.

This year, even the redcurrant plants stubbornly shed every little fruit that they managed to set. They did it systematically, deliberately, daily. Each afternoon she would find a hundred green berries on the ground.

What about the peaches, the Beale and the Bendigo? Her nursery man had assured her all those long years ago when the garden was young. Perfect for your garden, trees not too big, you'll have an early crop and a late crop, they mature at different times, he had told her. What her nursery man had not known was that the neighbours' trees cast such shadows that the peach trees, competing for light, had grown so high and it was impossible to harvest the meagre output.

This year, miraculously, there was a promise of a few more plush peaches within reach. Yes they had survived the spring chills, the curly leaf, the thrip infestation, the flood and now the drought. They were getting plumper every day. Maybe there was a sign of hope, of some fecundity at this place, and her hopeful, superstitious self thought that, just perhaps, one of the girls would be ... who knows?

One morning, Mary heard a loud noise coming from the garden, as if someone was breaking large sticks of wood, and to her horror, she saw a flock of white cockatoos retreating as they heard the backdoor creak open. All over the ground were the remains of dozens, hundreds, of walnuts. But not only that, every single peach had been *half* eaten and, as if disdainfully, cast away on the ground. She remembered a wheat farmer in the Western District who used to have most of his crop devoured by birds. I just shoot the bastards, he had told her. She recalled the horror she had felt hearing him say those words. 'Now I can well understand how he felt,' she told herself loudly. The bastards.

Why did each episode of lost fruit fling her even further into a pit of depression? Why was she becoming so desperate as the summer days turned even more glorious and golden? I am an ungrateful wretch, she told herself, admiring the large bunches of grapes hanging lustily from the vine twining around the pergola. How can I not be happy seeing this miracle? Yes, this year the grapes were plump and numerous, so at least something was working for her. In the past she had never tasted them. The birds ate every single one of them and she had not resented that.

But this year, some treacherous, negative, mean-spirited impulse made her cover every single bunch of grapes with a brown paper bag. At least this gave her something to hope for, she told herself, I can save some of these bunches for when the children come for dinner next time.

One day, as she was placing the last few paper bags around the bunches, to her great delight, she found a nest with three bird's eggs inside. They were blue and speckled and warm to touch. When the mother bird saw her up the ladder, she flew away squawking and protesting violently at the intrusion.

Each day Mary furtively watched the progress of the little baby birds, when their mother was away somewhere else digging up worms. After several days the featherless creatures turned from tiny transparent bags of food to squealing, assertive little creatures with fluffy wings.

'Wonderful, wonderful,' she said with a chuckle, as she put the little fledglings gently back in the nest.

'I'm not going to harm your little bubbies!' and to reassure the mother bird, who had come to watch her from a nearby tree, she moved the ladder away. The bird stopped its shrill protests and flew back into her nest.

But as Mary got distracted watching the bird, she slipped, and the ladder fell on her.

'Shit, shit, that's all I need!'

Screaming, she had found herself lying on a prickly pear bush. When someone had given her that plant, Mary had placed it in a neglected part of the garden away from any traffic. She realised now that she was covered with thorns. Tears of excruciating pain were rolling down her cheeks. There was no one around, thankfully, and she found some relief as she yelled and cried and howled and carried on like a mad woman, while trying to remove the thorns from her flesh.

Ashamed, she calmed down after a few minutes, and looking closer at that neglected part of her garden, she saw something that made her heart leap for joy: a clump of tuberoses which had never flowered since she had planted them years before.

Tuberoses, perfumed and gorgeous. Once she had been to a wedding, where money had married money, and there were ten thousand tuberoses, ten thousand spikes, all imported, naturally. The perfume was overpowering, and when the sun set, in the light of the candles strategically placed along the marquee, they appeared like glittering, multilayered stars.

And now, among the weeds, she had discovered a dozen spikes of plump white buds with a light pink tinge at the edges. At last, at long last, those plants, those wonderful plants with their bewitching perfume, were coming into flower quietly, surreptitiously, just when she had almost given up hope.

Mary's tears of pain turned into tears of joy. Maybe those flowers of fecundity were an omen of some impending good news.